AF514087

Marx Machiavelli Chesterton Emerson Joyce
Abbott Hardy Montaigne Cooper Austen
Defoe Melville Haggard Hugo
Christie Carroll Eliot Grimm
Stoker Molière
Wilde Maupassant Byron
Engels Schiller
Garnett Einstein Fitzgerald Smith
Goethe Hawthorne Kafka
Cotton Dostoyevsky Hall
Baum Kipling Doyle Willis
Leslie Dumas Henry Nietzsche
Flaubert Turgenev Balzac
Stockton Vatsyayana Crane
Burroughs Whitman Verne
Curtis Tocqueville Gogol Vinci
Homer Widger Tolstoy Busch
Darwin Thoreau
Potter Freud Zola Twain Plato Scott
Lawrence
Kant Jowett Stevenson Dickens
Andersen Cervantes Burton Hesse Harte
London Descartes
Poe Aristotle Wells Voltaire
Hale James Hastings
Bunner Shakespeare Cooke
Richter Chekhov Chambers Irving
Doré da Shaw Wodehouse Benedict
Swift Dante Alcott
Pushkin
Newton

tredition®

tredition was established in 2006 by Sandra Latusseck and Soenke Schulz. Based in Hamburg, Germany, tredition offers publishing solutions to authors and publishing houses, combined with worldwide distribution of printed and digital book content. tredition is uniquely positioned to enable authors and publishing houses to create books on their own terms and without conventional manufacturing risks.

For more information please visit: www.tredition.com

TREDITION CLASSICS

This book is part of the TREDITION CLASSICS series. The creators of this series are united by passion for literature and driven by the intention of making all public domain books available in printed format again - worldwide. Most TREDITION CLASSICS titles have been out of print and off the bookstore shelves for decades. At tredition we believe that a great book never goes out of style and that its value is eternal. Several mostly non-profit literature projects provide content to tredition. To support their good work, tredition donates a portion of the proceeds from each sold copy. As a reader of a TREDITION CLASSICS book, you support our mission to save many of the amazing works of world literature from oblivion. See all available books at www.tredition.com.

Project Gutenberg

The content for this book has been graciously provided by Project Gutenberg. Project Gutenberg is a non-profit organization founded by Michael Hart in 1971 at the University of Illinois. The mission of Project Gutenberg is simple: To encourage the creation and distribution of eBooks. Project Gutenberg is the first and largest collection of public domain eBooks.

Enoch Arden, &c.

Alfred Tennyson, Baron Tennyson

Imprint

This book is part of TREDITION CLASSICS

Author: Alfred Tennyson, Baron Tennyson
Cover design: Buchgut, Berlin – Germany

Publisher: tredition GmbH, Hamburg - Germany
ISBN: 978-3-8424-3939-9

www.tredition.com
www.tredition.de

The intention of the TREDITION CLASSICS series is to make world literature in the public domain available in printed format. Literary enthusiasts and organizations, such as Project Gutenberg, worldwide have scanned and digitally edited the original texts. tredition has subsequently formatted and redesigned the content into a modern reading layout. Therefore, we cannot guarantee the exact reproduction of the original format of a particular historic edition. Please also note that no modifications have been made to the spelling, therefore it may differ from the orthography used today.

ENOCH ARDEN, &c.

by ALFRED TENNYSON.

CONTENTS

ENOCH ARDEN.

Long lines of cliff breaking have left a chasm;
And in the chasm are foam and yellow sands;
Beyond, red roofs about a narrow wharf
In cluster; then a moulder'd church; and higher
A long street climbs to one tall-tower'd mill;
And high in heaven behind it a gray down
With Danish barrows; and a hazelwood,
By autumn nutters haunted, flourishes
Green in a cuplike hollow of the down.

Here on this beach a hundred years ago,
Three children of three houses, Annie Lee,
The prettiest little damsel in the port,
And Philip Ray the miller's only son,
And Enoch Arden, a rough sailor's lad
Made orphan by a winter shipwreck, play'd
Among the waste and lumber of the shore,
Hard coils of cordage, swarthy fishing-nets,
Anchors of rusty fluke, and boats updrawn,
And built their castles of dissolving sand
To watch them overflow'd, or following up
And flying the white breaker, daily left
The little footprint daily wash'd away.

A narrow cave ran in beneath the cliff:
In this the children play'd at keeping house.
Enoch was host one day, Philip the next,
While Annie still was mistress; but at times
Enoch would hold possession for a week:
'This is my house and this my little wife.'
'Mine too' said Philip 'turn and turn about:'
When, if they quarrell'd, Enoch stronger-made

Was master: then would Philip, his blue eyes
All flooded with the helpless wrath of tears,
Shriek out 'I hate you, Enoch,' and at this
The little wife would weep for company,
And pray them not to quarrel for her sake,
And say she would be little wife to both.

But when the dawn of rosy childhood past,
And the new warmth of life's ascending sun
Was felt by either, either fixt his heart
On that one girl; and Enoch spoke his love,
But Philip loved in silence; and the girl
Seem'd kinder unto Philip than to him;
But she loved Enoch; tho' she knew it not,
And would if ask'd deny it. Enoch set
A purpose evermore before his eyes,
To hoard all savings to the uttermost,
To purchase his own boat, and make a home
For Annie: and so prosper'd that at last
A luckier or a bolder fisherman,
A carefuller in peril, did not breathe
For leagues along that breaker-beaten coast
Than Enoch. Likewise had he served a year
On board a merchantman, and made himself
Full sailor; and he thrice had pluck'd a life
From the dread sweep of the down-streaming seas:
And all me look'd upon him favorably:
And ere he touch'd his one-and-twentieth May
He purchased his own boat, and made a home
For Annie, neat and nestlike, halfway up
The narrow street that clamber'd toward the mill.

Then, on a golden autumn eventide,
The younger people making holiday,
With bag and sack and basket, great and small,
Went nutting to the hazels. Philip stay'd
(His father lying sick and needing him)
An hour behind; but as he climb'd the hill,

Just where the prone edge of the wood began
To feather toward the hollow, saw the pair,
Enoch and Annie, sitting hand-in-hand,
His large gray eyes and weather-beaten face
All-kindled by a still and sacred fire,
That burn'd as on an altar. Philip look'd,
And in their eyes and faces read his doom;
Then, as their faces drew together, groan'd,
And slipt aside, and like a wounded life
Crept down into the hollows of the wood;
There, while the rest were loud in merrymaking,
Had his dark hour unseen, and rose and past
Bearing a lifelong hunger in his heart.

So these were wed, and merrily rang the bells,
And merrily ran the years, seven happy years,
Seven happy years of health and competence,
And mutual love and honorable toil;
With children; first a daughter. In him woke,
With his first babe's first cry, the noble wish
To save all earnings to the uttermost,
And give his child a better bringing-up
Than his had been, or hers; a wish renew'd,
When two years after came a boy to be
The rosy idol of her solitudes,
While Enoch was abroad on wrathful seas,
Or often journeying landward; for in truth
Enoch's white horse, and Enoch's ocean-spoil
In ocean-smelling osier, and his face,
Rough-redden'd with a thousand winter gales,
Not only to the market-cross were known,
But in the leafy lanes behind the down,
Far as the portal-warding lion-whelp,
And peacock-yewtree of the lonely Hall,
Whose Friday fare was Enoch's ministering.

Then came a change, as all things human change.
Ten miles to northward of the narrow port

Open'd a larger haven: thither used
Enoch at times to go by land or sea;
And once when there, and clambering on a mast
In harbor, by mischance he slipt and fell:
A limb was broken when they lifted him;
And while he lay recovering there, his wife
Bore him another son, a sickly one:
Another hand crept too across his trade
Taking her bread and theirs: and on him fell,
Altho' a grave and staid God-fearing man,
Yet lying thus inactive, doubt and gloom.
He seem'd, as in a nightmare of the night,
To see his children leading evermore
Low miserable lives of hand-to-mouth,
And her, he loved, a beggar: then he pray'd
'Save them from this, whatever comes to me.'
And while he pray'd, the master of that ship
Enoch had served in, hearing his mischance,
Came, for he knew the man and valued him,
Reporting of his vessel China-bound,
And wanting yet a boatswain. Would he go?
There yet were many weeks before she sail'd,
Sail'd from this port. Would Enoch have the place?
And Enoch all at once assented to it,
Rejoicing at that answer to his prayer.

So now that the shadow of mischance appear'd
No graver than as when some little cloud
Cuts off the fiery highway of the sun,
And isles a light in the offing: yet the wife—
When he was gone—the children—what to do?
Then Enoch lay long-pondering on his plans;
To sell the boat—and yet he loved her well—
How many a rough sea had he weather'd in her!
He knew her, as a horseman knows his horse—
And yet to sell her—then with what she brought
Buy goods and stores—set Annie forth in trade
With all that seamen needed or their wives—

So might she keep the house while he was gone.
Should he not trade himself out yonder? go
This voyage more than once? yea twice or thrice—
As oft as needed—last, returning rich,
Become the master of a larger craft,
With fuller profits lead an easier life,
Have all his pretty young ones educated,
And pass his days in peace among his own.

Thus Enoch in his heart determined all:
Then moving homeward came on Annie pale,
Nursing the sickly babe, her latest-born.
Forward she started with a happy cry,
And laid the feeble infant in his arms;
Whom Enoch took, and handled all his limbs,
Appraised his weight and fondled fatherlike,
But had no heart to break his purposes
To Annie, till the morrow, when he spoke.

Then first since Enoch's golden ring had girt
Her finger, Annie fought against his will:
Yet not with brawling opposition she,
But manifold entreaties, many a tear,
Many a sad kiss by day and night renew'd
(Sure that all evil would come out of it)
Besought him, supplicating, if he cared
For here or his dear children, not to go.
He not for his own self caring but her,
Her and her children, let her plead in vain;
So grieving held his will, and bore it thro'.

For Enoch parted with his old sea-friend,
Bought Annie goods and stores, and set his hand
To fit their little streetward sitting-room
With shelf and corner for the goods and stores.
So all day long till Enoch's last at home,
Shaking their pretty cabin, hammer and axe,

Auger and saw, while Annie seem'd to hear
Her own death-scaffold raising, shrill'd and rang,
Till this was ended, and his careful hand,—
The space was narrow,—having order'd all
Almost as neat and close as Nature packs
Her blossom or her seedling, paused; and he,
Who needs would work for Annie to the last,
Ascending tired, heavily slept till morn.

And Enoch faced this morning of farewell
Brightly and boldly. All his Annie's fears,
Save, as his Annie's, were a laughter to him.
Yet Enoch as a brave God-fearing man
Bow'd himself down, and in that mystery
Where God-in-man is one with man-in-God,
Pray'd for a blessing on his wife and babes
Whatever came to him: and then he said
'Annie, this voyage by the grace of God
Will bring fair weather yet to all of us.
Keep a clean hearth and a clear fire for me,
For I'll be back, my girl, before you know it.'
Then lightly rocking baby's cradle 'and he,
This pretty, puny, weakly little one,—
Nay—for I love him all the better for it—
God bless him, he shall sit upon my knees
And I will tell him tales of foreign parts,
And make him merry, when I come home again.
Come Annie, come, cheer up before I go.'

Him running on thus hopefully she heard,
And almost hoped herself; but when he turn'd
The current of his talk to graver things
In sailor fashion roughly sermonizing
On providence and trust in Heaven, she heard,
Heard and not heard him; as the village girl,
Who sets her pitcher underneath the spring,
Musing on him that used to fill it for her,

Hears and not hears, and lets it overflow.

At length she spoke 'O Enoch, you are wise;
And yet for all your wisdom well know I
That I shall look upon your face no more.'

'Well then,' said Enoch, 'I shall look on yours.
Annie, the ship I sail in passes here
(He named the day) get you a seaman's glass,
Spy out my face, and laugh at all your fears.'

But when the last of those last moments came,
'Annie my girl, cheer up, be comforted,
Look to the babes, and till I come again,
Keep everything shipshape, for I must go.
And fear no more for me; or if you fear
Cast all your cares on God; that anchor holds.
Is He not yonder in those uttermost
Parts of the morning? if I flee to these
Can I go from Him? and the sea is His,
The sea is His: He made it.'

Enoch rose,
Cast his strong arms about his drooping wife,
And kiss'd his wonder-stricken little ones;
But for the third, sickly one, who slept
After a night of feverous wakefulness,
When Annie would have raised him Enoch said
'Wake him not; let him sleep; how should this child
Remember this?' and kiss'ed him in his cot.
But Annie from her baby's forehead clipt
A tiny curl, and gave it: this he kept
Thro' all his future; but now hastily caught
His bundle, waved his hand, and went his way.

She when the day, that Enoch mention'd, came,
Borrow'd a glass, but all in vain: perhaps
She could not fix the glass to suit her eye;
Perhaps her eye was dim, hand tremulous;
She saw him not: and while he stood on deck
Waving, the moment and the vessel past.

Ev'n to the last dip of the vanishing sail
She watch'd it, and departed weeping for him;
Then, tho' she mourn'd his absence as his grave,
Set her sad will no less to chime with his,
But throve not in her trade, not being bred
To barter, nor compensating the want
By shrewdness, neither capable of lies,
Nor asking overmuch and taking less,
And still foreboding 'what would Enoch say?'
For more than once, in days of difficulty
And pressure, had she sold her wares for less
Than what she gave in buying what she sold:
She fail'd and sadden'd knowing it; and thus,
Expectant of that news that never came,
Gain'd for here own a scanty sustenance,
And lived a life of silent melancholy.

Now the third child was sickly-born and grew
Yet sicklier, tho' the mother cared for it
With all a mother's care: nevertheless,
Whether her business often call'd her from it,
Or thro' the want of what it needed most,
Or means to pay the voice who best could tell
What most it needed—howsoe'er it was,
After a lingering,—ere she was aware,—
Like the caged bird escaping suddenly,
The little innocent soul flitted away.

In that same week when Annie buried it,
Philip's true heart, which hunger'd for her peace

(Since Enoch left he had not look'd upon her),
Smote him, as having kept aloof so long.
'Surely' said Philip 'I may see her now,
May be some little comfort;' therefore went,
Past thro' the solitary room in front,
Paused for a moment at an inner door,
Then struck it thrice, and, no one opening,
Enter'd; but Annie, seated with her grief,
Fresh from the burial of her little one,
Cared not to look on any human face,
But turn'd her own toward the wall and wept.
Then Philip standing up said falteringly
'Annie, I came to ask a favor of you.'

He spoke; the passion in her moan'd reply
'Favor from one so sad and so forlorn
As I am!' half abash'd him; yet unask'd,
His bashfulness and tenderness at war,
He set himself beside her, saying to her:

'I came to speak to you of what he wish'd,
Enoch, your husband: I have ever said
You chose the best among us—a strong man:
For where he fixt his heart he set his hand
To do the thing he will'd, and bore it thro'.
And wherefore did he go this weary way,
And leave you lonely? not to see the world—
For pleasure?—nay, but for the wherewithal
To give his babes a better bringing-up
Than his had been, or yours: that was his wish.
And if he come again, vext will he be
To find the precious morning hours were lost.
And it would vex him even in his grave,
If he could know his babes were running wild
Like colts about the waste. So Annie, now—
Have we not known each other all our lives?
I do beseech you by the love you bear
Him and his children not to say me nay—

For, if you will, when Enoch comes again
Why then he shall repay me—if you will,
Annie—for I am rich and well-to-do.
Now let me put the boy and girl to school:
This is the favor that I came to ask.'

Then Annie with her brows against the wall
Answer'd 'I cannot look you in the face;
I seem so foolish and so broken down.
When you came in my sorrow broke me down;
And now I think your kindness breaks me down;
But Enoch lives; that is borne in on me:
He will repay you: money can be repaid;
Not kindness such as yours.'

And Philip ask'd
'Then you will let me, Annie?'

There she turn'd,
She rose, and fixt her swimming eyes upon him,
And dwelt a moment on his kindly face,
Then calling down a blessing on his head
Caught at his hand and wrung it passionately,
And past into the little garth beyond.
So lifted up in spirit he moved away.

Then Philip put the boy and girl to school,
And bought them needful books, and everyway,
Like one who does his duty by his own,
Made himself theirs; and tho' for Annie's sake,
Fearing the lazy gossip of the port,
He oft denied his heart his dearest wish,
And seldom crost her threshold, yet he sent
Gifts by the children, garden-herbs and fruit,
The late and early roses from his wall,
Or conies from the down, and now and then,
With some pretext of fineness in the meal

To save the offence of charitable, flour
From his tall mill that whistled on the waste.

But Philip did not fathom Annie's mind:
Scarce could the woman when he came upon her,
Out of full heart and boundless gratitude
Light on a broken word to thank him with.
But Philip was her children's all-in-all;
From distant corners of the street they ran
To greet his hearty welcome heartily;
Lords of his house and of his mill were they;
Worried his passive ear with petty wrongs
Or pleasures, hung upon him, play'd with him
And call'd him Father Philip. Philip gain'd
As Enoch lost; for Enoch seem'd to them
Uncertain as a vision or a dream,
Faint as a figure seen in early dawn
Down at the far end of an avenue,
Going we know not where: and so ten years,
Since Enoch left his hearth and native land,
Fled forward, and no news of Enoch came.

It chanced one evening Annie's children long'd
To go with others, nutting to the wood,
And Annie would go with them; then they begg'd
For Father Philip (as they call'd him) too:
Him, like the working bee in blossom-dust,
Blanch'd with his mill, they found; and saying to him
'Come with us Father Philip' he denied;
But when the children pluck'd at him to go,
He laugh'd, and yielding readily to their wish,
For was not Annie with them? and they went.

But after scaling half the weary down,
Just where the prone edge of the wood began
To feather toward the hollow, all her force
Fail'd her; and sighing 'let me rest' she said.

So Philip rested with her well-content;
While all the younger ones with jubilant cries
Broke from their elders, and tumultuously
Down thro' the whitening hazels made a plunge
To the bottom, and dispersed, and beat or broke
The lithe reluctant boughs to tear away
Their tawny clusters, crying to each other
And calling, here and there, about the wood.

But Philip sitting at her side forgot
Her presence, and remember'd one dark hour
Here in this wood, when like a wounded life
He crept into the shadow: at last he said
Lifting his honest forehead 'Listen, Annie,
How merry they are down yonder in the wood.'
'Tired, Annie?' for she did not speak a word.
'Tired?' but her face had fall'n upon her hands;
At which, as with a kind anger in him,
'The ship was lost' he said 'the ship was lost!
No more of that! why should you kill yourself
And make them orphans quite?' And Annie said
'I thought not of it: but—I known not why—
Their voices make me feel so solitary.'

Then Philip coming somewhat closer spoke.
'Annie, there is a thing upon my mind,
And it has been upon my mind so long,
That tho' I know not when it first came there,
I know that it will out at last. O Annie,
It is beyond all hope, against all chance,
That he who left you ten long years ago
Should still be living; well then—let me speak:
I grieve to see you poor and wanting help:
I cannot help you as I wish to do
Unless—they say that women are so quick—
Perhaps you know what I would have you know—
I wish you for my wife. I fain would prove
A father to your children: I do think

They love me as a father: I am sure
That I love them as if they were mine own;
And I believe, if you were fast my wife,
That after all these sad uncertain years,
We might be still as happy as God grants
To any of His creatures. Think upon it:
For I am well-to-do — no kin, no care,
No burthen, save my care for you and yours:
And we have known each other all our lives,
And I have loved you longer than you know.'

Then answer'd Annie; tenderly she spoke:
'You have been as God's good angel in our house.
God bless you for it, God reward you for it,
Philip, with something happier than myself.
Can one live twice? can you be ever loved
As Enoch was? what is it that you ask?'
'I am content' he answer'd 'to be loved
A little after Enoch.' 'O' she cried
Scared as it were 'dear Philip, wait a while:
If Enoch comes — but Enoch will not come —
Yet wait a year, a year is not so long:
Surely I shall be wiser in a year:
O wait a little!' Philip sadly said
'Annie, as I have waited all my life
I well may wait a little.' 'Nay' she cried
'I am bound: you have my promise — in a year:
Will you not bide your year as I bide mine?'
And Philip answer'd 'I will bide my year.'

Here both were mute, till Philip glancing up
Beheld the dead flame of the fallen day
Pass from the Danish barrow overhead;
Then fearing night and chill for Annie rose,
And sent his voice beneath him thro' the wood.
Up came the children laden with their spoil;
Then all descended to the port, and there
At Annie's door he paused and gave his hand,

Saying gently 'Annie, when I spoke to you,
That was your hour of weakness. I was wrong.
I am always bound to you, but you are free.'
Then Annie weeping answer'd 'I am bound.'

She spoke; and in one moment as it were,
While yet she went about her household ways,
Ev'n as she dwelt upon his latest words,
That he had loved her longer than she knew,
That autumn into autumn flash'd again,
And there he stood once more before her face,
Claiming her promise. 'Is it a year?' she ask'd.
'Yes, if the nuts' he said 'be ripe again:
Come out and see.' But she—she put him off—
So much to look to—such a change—a month—
Give her a month—she knew that she was bound—
A month—no more. Then Philip with his eyes
Full of that lifelong hunger, and his voice
Shaking a little like a drunkard's hand,
'Take your own time, Annie, take your own time.'
And Annie could have wept for pity of him;
And yet she held him on delayingly
With many a scarce-believable excuse,
Trying his truth and his long-sufferance,
Till half-another year had slipt away.

By this the lazy gossips of the port,
Abhorrent of a calculation crost,
Began to chafe as at a personal wrong.
Some thought that Philip did but trifle with her;
Some that she but held off to draw him on;
And others laugh'd at her and Philip too,
As simple folks that knew not their own minds;
And one, in whom all evil fancies clung
Like serpent eggs together, laughingly
Would hint a worse in either. Her own son
Was silent, tho' he often look'd his wish;
But evermore the daughter prest upon her

To wed the man so dear to all of them
And lift the household out of poverty;
And Philip's rosy face contracting grew
Careworn and wan; and all these things fell on her
Sharp as reproach.

At last one night it chanced
That Annie could not sleep, but earnestly
Pray'd for a sign 'my Enoch is he gone?'
Then compass'd round by the blind wall of night
Brook'd not the expectant terror of her heart,
Started from bed, and struck herself a light,
Then desperately seized the holy Book,
Suddenly set it wide to find a sign,
Suddenly put her finger on the text,
'Under a palmtree.' That was nothing to her:
No meaning there: she closed the book and slept:
When lo! her Enoch sitting on a height,
Under a palmtree, over him the Sun:
'He is gone' she thought 'he is happy, he is singing
Hosanna in the highest: yonder shines
The Sun of Righteousness, and these be palms
Whereof the happy people strowing cried
"Hosanna in the highest!"' Here she woke,
Resolved, sent for him and said wildly to him
'There is no reason why we should not wed.'
'Then for God's sake,' he answer'd, 'both our sakes,
So you will wed me, let it be at once.'

So these were wed and merrily rang the bells,
Merrily rang the bells and they were wed.
But never merrily beat Annie's heart.
A footstep seem'd to fall beside her path,
She knew not whence; a whisper in her ear,
She knew not what; nor loved she to be left
Alone at home, nor ventured out alone.
What ail'd her then, that ere she enter'd, often
Her hand dwelt lingeringly on the latch,

Fearing to enter: Philip thought he knew:
Such doubts and fears were common to her state,
Being with child: but when her child was born,
Then her new child was as herself renew'd,
Then the new mother came about her heart,
Then her good Philip was her all-in-all,
And that mysterious instinct wholly died.

And where was Enoch? prosperously sail'd
The ship 'Good Fortune,' tho' at setting forth
The Biscay, roughly ridging eastward, shook
And almost overwhelm'd her, yet unvext
She slipt across the summer of the world,
Then after a long tumble about the Cape
And frequent interchange of foul and fair,
She passing thro' the summer world again,
The breath of heaven came continually
And sent her sweetly by the golden isles,
Till silent in her oriental haven.

There Enoch traded for himself, and bought
Quaint monsters for the market of those times,
A gilded dragon, also, for the babes.

Less lucky her home-voyage: at first indeed
Thro' many a fair sea-circle, day by day,
Scarce-rocking, her full-busted figure-head
Stared o'er the ripple feathering from her bows:
Then follow'd calms, and then winds variable,
Then baffling, a long course of them; and last
Storm, such as drove her under moonless heavens
Till hard upon the cry of 'breakers' came
The crash of ruin, and the loss of all
But Enoch and two others. Half the night,
Buoy'd upon floating tackle and broken spars,
These drifted, stranding on an isle at morn

Rich, but loneliest in a lonely sea.

No want was there of human sustenance,
Soft fruitage, mighty nuts, and nourishing roots;
Nor save for pity was it hard to take
The helpless life so wild that it was tame.
There in a seaward-gazing mountain-gorge
They built, and thatch'd with leaves of palm, a hut,
Half hut, half native cavern. So the three,
Set in this Eden of all plenteousness,
Dwelt with eternal summer, ill-content.

For one, the youngest, hardly more than boy,
Hurt in that night of sudden ruin and wreck,
Lay lingering out a three-years' death-in-life.
They could not leave him. After he was gone,
The two remaining found a fallen stem;
And Enoch's comrade, careless of himself,
Fire-hollowing this in Indian fashion, fell
Sun-stricken, and that other lived alone.
In those two deaths he read God's warning 'wait.'

The mountain wooded to the peak, the lawns
And winding glades high up like ways to Heaven,
The slender coco's drooping crown of plumes,
The lightning flash of insect and of bird,
The lustre of the long convolvuluses
That coil'd around the stately stems, and ran
Ev'n to the limit of the land, the glows
And glories of the broad belt of the world,
All these he saw; but what he fain had seen
He could not see, the kindly human face,
Nor ever hear a kindly voice, but heard
The myriad shriek of wheeling ocean-fowl,
The league-long roller thundering on the reef,
The moving whisper of huge trees that branch'd
And blossom'd in the zenith, or the sweep

Of some precipitous rivulet to the wave,
As down the shore he ranged, or all day long
Sat often in the seaward-gazing gorge,
A shipwreck'd sailor, waiting for a sail:
No sail from day to day, but every day
The sunrise broken into scarlet shafts
Among the palms and ferns and precipices;
The blaze upon the waters to the east;
The blaze upon his island overhead;
The blaze upon the waters to the west;
Then the great stars that globed themselves in Heaven,
The hollower-bellowing ocean, and again
The scarlet shafts of sunrise—but no sail.

There often as he watch'd or seem'd to watch,
So still, the golden lizard on him paused,
A phantom made of many phantoms moved
Before him haunting him, or he himself
Moved haunting people, things and places, known
Far in a darker isle beyond the line;
The babes, their babble, Annie, the small house,
The climbing street, the mill, the leafy lanes,
The peacock-yewtree and the lonely Hall,
The horse he drove, the boat he sold, the chill
November dawns and dewy-glooming downs,
The gentle shower, the smell of dying leaves,
And the low moan of leaden-color'd seas.

Once likewise, in the ringing of his ears,
Tho' faintly, merrily—far and far away—
He heard the pealing of his parish bells;
Then, tho' he knew not wherefore, started up
Shuddering, and when the beauteous hateful isle
Return'd upon him, had not his poor heart
Spoken with That, which being everywhere
Lets none, who speaks with Him, seem all alone,
Surely the man had died of solitude.

Thus over Enoch's early-silvering head
The sunny and rainy seasons came and went
Year after year. His hopes to see his own,
And pace the sacred old familiar fields,
Not yet had perish'd, when his lonely doom
Came suddenly to an end. Another ship
(She wanted water) blown by baffling winds,
Like the Good Fortune, from her destined course,
Stay'd by this isle, not knowing where she lay:
For since the mate had seen at early dawn
Across a break on the mist-wreathen isle
The silent water slipping from the hills,
They sent a crew that landing burst away
In search of stream or fount, and fill'd the shores
With clamor. Downward from his mountain gorge
Stept the long-hair'd long-bearded solitary,
Brown, looking hardly human, strangely clad,
Muttering and mumbling, idiotlike it seem'd,
With inarticulate rage, and making signs
They knew not what: and yet he led the way
To where the rivulets of sweet water ran;
And ever as he mingled with the crew,
And heard them talking, his long-bounden tongue
Was loosen'd, till he made them understand;
Whom, when their casks were fill'd they took aboard:
And there the tale he utter'd brokenly,
Scarce credited at first but more and more,
Amazed and melted all who listen'd to it:
And clothes they gave him and free passage home;
But oft he work'd among the rest and shook
His isolation from him. None of these
Came from his county, or could answer him,
If question'd, aught of what he cared to know.
And dull the voyage was with long delays,
The vessel scarce sea-worthy; but evermore
His fancy fled before the lazy wind
Returning, till beneath a clouded moon
He like a lover down thro' all his blood
Drew in the dewy meadowy morning-breath

Of England, blown across her ghostly wall:
And that same morning officers and men
Levied a kindly tax upon themselves,
Pitying the lonely man, and gave him it:
Then moving up the coast they landed him,
Ev'n in that harbor whence he sail'd before.

There Enoch spoke no word to anyone,
But homeward—home—what home? had he a home?
His home, he walk'd. Bright was that afternoon,
Sunny but chill; till drawn thro' either chasm,
Where either haven open'd on the deeps,
Roll'd a sea-haze and whelm'd the world in gray;
Cut off the length of highway on before,
And left but narrow breadth to left and right
Of wither'd holt or tilth or pasturage.
On the nigh-naked tree the Robin piped
Disconsolate, and thro' the dripping haze
The dead weight of the dead leaf bore it down.
Thicker the drizzle grew, deeper the gloom;
Last, as it seem'd, a great mist-blotted light
Flared on him, and he came upon the place.

Then down the long street having slowly stolen,
His heart foreshadowing all calamity,
His eyes upon the stones, he reach'd the home
Where Annie lived and loved him, and his babes
In those far-off seven happy years were born;
But finding neither light nor murmur there
(A bill of sale gleam'd thro' the drizzle) crept
Still downward thinking 'dead or dead to me!'

Down to the pool and narrow wharf he went,
Seeking a tavern which of old he knew,
A front of timber-crost antiquity,
So propt, worm-eaten, ruinously old,
He thought it must have gone; but he was gone

Who kept it; and his widow, Miriam Lane,
With daily-dwindling profits held the house;
A haunt of brawling seamen once, but now
Stiller, with yet a bed for wandering men.
There Enoch rested silently many days.

But Miriam Lane was good and garrulous,
Nor let him be, but often breaking in,
Told him, with other annals of the port,
Not knowing—Enoch was so brown, so bow'd,
So broken—all the story of his house.
His baby's death, her growing poverty,
How Philip put her little ones to school,
And kept them in it, his long wooing her,
Her slow consent, and marriage, and the birth
Of Philip's child: and o'er his countenance
No shadow past, nor motion: anyone,
Regarding, well had deem'd he felt the tale
Less than the teller: only when she closed
'Enoch, poor man, was cast away and lost'
He, shaking his gray head pathetically,
Repeated muttering 'cast away and lost;'
Again in deeper inward whispers 'lost!'

But Enoch yearn'd to see her face again;
'If I might look on her sweet face gain
And know that she is happy.' So the thought
Haunted and harass'd him, and drove him forth,
At evening when the dull November day
Was growing duller twilight, to the hill.
There he sat down gazing on all below;
There did a thousand memories roll upon him,
Unspeakable for sadness. By and by
The ruddy square of comfortable light,
Far blazing from the rear of Philip's house,
Allured him, as the beacon-blaze allures
The bird of passage, till he madly strikes

Against it, and beats out his weary life.

For Philip's dwelling fronted on the street,
The latest house to landward; but behind,
With one small gate that open'd on the waste,
Flourish'd a little garden square and wall'd:
And in it throve an ancient evergreen,
A yewtree, and all round it ran a walk
Of shingle, and a walk divided it:
But Enoch shunn'd the middle walk and stole
Up by the wall, behind the yew; and thence
That which he better might have shunn'd, if griefs
Like his have worse or better, Enoch saw.

For cups and silver on the burnish'd board
Sparkled and shone; so genial was the hearth:
And on the right hand of the hearth he saw
Philip, the slighted suitor of old times,
Stout, rosy, with his babe across his knees;
And o'er her second father stoopt a girl,
A later but a loftier Annie Lee,
Fair-hair'd and tall, and from her lifted hand
Dangled a length of ribbon and a ring
To tempt the babe, who rear'd his creasy arms,
Caught at and ever miss'd it, and they laugh'd:
And on the left hand of the hearth he saw
The mother glancing often toward her babe,
But turning now and then to speak with him,
Her son, who stood beside her tall and strong,
And saying that which pleased him, for he smiled.

Now when the dead man come to life beheld
His wife his wife no more, and saw the babe
Hers, yet not his, upon the father's knee,
And all the warmth, the peace, the happiness,
And his own children tall and beautiful,
And him, that other, reigning in his place,

Lord of his rights and of his children's love,—
Then he, tho' Miriam Lane had told him all,
Because things seen are mightier than things heard,
Stagger'd and shook, holding the branch, and fear'd
To send abroad a shrill and terrible cry,
Which in one moment, like the blast of doom,
Would shatter all the happiness of the hearth.

He therefore turning softly like a thief,
Lest the harsh shingle should grate underfoot,
And feeling all along the garden-wall,
Lest he should swoon and tumble and be found,
Crept to the gate, and open'd it, and closed,
As lightly as a sick man's chamber-door,
Behind him, and came out upon the waste.

And there he would have knelt, but that his knees
Were feeble, so that falling prone he dug
His fingers into the wet earth, and pray'd.

'Too hard to bear! why did they take me hence?
O God Almighty, blessed Saviour, Thou
That didst uphold me on my lonely isle,
Uphold me, Father, in my loneliness
A little longer! aid me, give me strength
Not to tell her, never to let her know.
Help me no to break in upon her peace.
My children too! must I not speak to these?
They know me not. I should betray myself.
Never: not father's kiss for me—the girl
So like her mother, and the boy, my son.'

There speech and thought and nature fail'd a little,
And he lay tranced; but when he rose and paced
Back toward his solitary home again,
All down the long and narrow street he went
Beating it in upon his weary brain,

As tho' it were the burthen of a song,
'Not to tell her, never to let her know.'

He was not all unhappy. His resolve
Upbore him, and firm faith, and evermore
Prayer from a living source within the will,
And beating up thro' all the bitter world,
Like fountains of sweet water in the sea,
Kept him a living soul. 'This miller's wife'
He said to Miriam 'that you told me of,
Has she no fear that her first husband lives?'
'Ay ay, poor soul' said Miriam, 'fear enow!
If you could tell her you had seen him dead,
Why, that would be her comfort;' and he thought
'After the Lord has call'd me she shall know,
I wait His time' and Enoch set himself,
Scorning an alms, to work whereby to live.
Almost to all things could he turn his hand.
Cooper he was and carpenter, and wrought
To make the boatmen fishing-nets, or help'd
At lading and unlading the tall barks,
That brought the stinted commerce of those days;
Thus earn'd a scanty living for himself:
Yet since he did but labor for himself,
Work without hope, there was not life in it
Whereby the man could live; and as the year
Roll'd itself round again to meet the day
When Enoch had return'd, a languor came
Upon him, gentle sickness, gradually
Weakening the man, till he could do no more,
But kept the house, his chair, and last his bed.
And Enoch bore his weakness cheerfully.
For sure no gladlier does the stranded wreck
See thro' the gray skirts of a lifting squall
The boat that bears the hope of life approach
To save the life despair'd of, than he saw
Death dawning on him, and the close of all.

For thro' that dawning gleam'd a kindlier hope
On Enoch thinking 'after I am gone,
Then may she learn I loved her to the last.'
He call'd aloud for Miriam Lane and said
'Woman, I have a secret—only swear,
Before I tell you—swear upon the book
Not to reveal it, till you see me dead.'
'Dead' clamor'd the good woman 'hear him talk!
I warrant, man, that we shall bring you round.'
'Swear' add Enoch sternly 'on the book.'
And on the book, half-frighted, Miriam swore.
Then Enoch rolling his gray eyes upon her,
'Did you know Enoch Arden of this town?'
'Know him?' she said 'I knew him far away.
Ay, ay, I mind him coming down the street;
Held his head high, and cared for no man, he.'
Slowly and sadly Enoch answer'd her;
'His head is low, and no man cares for him.
I think I have not three days more to live;
I am the man.' At which the woman gave
A half-incredulous, half-hysterical cry.
'You Arden, you! nay,—sure he was a foot
Higher than you be.' Enoch said again
'My God has bow'd me down to what I am;
My grief and solitude have broken me;
Nevertheless, know that I am he
Who married—but that name has twice been changed—
I married her who married Philip Ray.
Sit, listen.' Then he told her of his voyage,
His wreck, his lonely life, his coming back,
His gazing in on Annie, his resolve,
And how he kept it. As the woman heard,
Fast flow'd the current of her easy tears,
While in her heart she yearn'd incessantly
To rush abroad all round the little haven,
Proclaiming Enoch Arden and his woes;
But awed and promise-bounded she forbore,
Saying only 'See your bairns before you go!
Eh, let me fetch 'em, Arden,' and arose

Eager to bring them down, for Enoch hung
A moment on her words, but then replied.

'Woman, disturb me not now at the last,
But let me hold my purpose till I die.
Sit down again; mark me and understand,
While I have power to speak. I charge you now,
When you shall see her, tell her that I died
Blessing her, praying for her, loving her;
Save for the bar between us, loving her
As when she laid her head beside my own.
And tell my daughter Annie, whom I saw
So like her mother, that my latest breath
Was spent in blessing her and praying for her.
And tell my son that I died blessing him.
And say to Philip that I blest him too;
He never meant us any thing but good.
But if my children care to see me dead,
Who hardly saw me living, let them come,
I am their father; but she must not come,
For my dead face would vex her after-life.
And now there is but one of all my blood,
Who will embrace me in the world-to-be:
This hair is his: she cut it off and gave it,
And I have borne it with me all these years,
And thought to bear it with me to my grave;
But now my mind is changed, for I shall see him,
My babe in bliss: wherefore when I am gone,
Take, give her this, for it may comfort her:
It will moreover be a token to her,
That I am he.'

He ceased; and Miriam Lane
Made such a voluble answer promising all,
That once again he roll'd his eyes upon her
Repeating all he wish'd, and once again
She promised.

Then the third night after this,
While Enoch slumber'd motionless and pale,
And Miriam watch'd and dozed at intervals,
There came so loud a calling of the sea,
That all the houses in the haven rang.
He woke, he rose, he spread his arms abroad
Crying with a loud voice 'a sail! a sail!
I am saved'; and so fell back and spoke no more.

So past the strong heroic soul away.
And when they buried him the little port
Had seldom seen a costlier funeral.

AYLMER'S FIELD.
1793.

AYLMER'S FIELD.
1793.

– – –<>– – –

Dust are our frames; and gilded dust, our pride
Looks only for a moment whole and sound;
Like that long-buried body of the king,
Found lying with his urns and ornaments,
Which at a touch of light, an air of heaven,

Slipt into ashes and was found no more.

Here is a story which in rougher shape
Came from a grizzled cripple, whom I saw
Sunning himself in a waste field alone—
Old, and a mine of memories—who had served,
Long since, a bygone Rector of the place,
And been himself a part of what he told.

Sir Aylmer Aylmer that almighty man,
The county God—in whose capacious hall,
Hung with a hundred shields, the family tree
Sprang from the midriff of a prostrate king—
Whose blazing wyvern weathercock'd the spire,
Stood from his walls and wing'd his entry-gates
And swang besides on many a windy sign—
Whose eyes from under a pyramidal head
Saw from his windows nothing save his own—
What lovelier of his own had he than her,
His only child, his Edith, whom he loved
As heiress and not heir regretfully?
But 'he that marries her marries her name'
This fiat somewhat soothed himself and wife,
His wife a faded beauty of the Baths,
Insipid as the Queen upon a card;
Her all of thought and bearing hardly more
Than his own shadow in a sickly sun.

A land of hops and poppy-mingled corn,
Little about it stirring save a brook!
A sleepy land where under the same wheel
The same old rut would deepen year by year;
Where almost all the village had one name;
Where Aylmer follow'd Aylmer at the Hall
And Averill Averill at the Rectory
Thrice over; so that Rectory and Hall,
Bound in an immemorial intimacy,

Were open to each other; tho' to dream
That Love could bind them closer well had made
The hoar hair of the Baronet bristle up
With horror, worse than had he heard his priest
Preach an inverted scripture, sons of men
Daughters of God; so sleepy was the land.

And might not Averill, had he will'd it so,
Somewhere beneath his own low range of roofs,
Have also set his many-shielded tree?
There was an Aylmer-Averill marriage once,
When the red rose was redder than itself,
And York's white rose as red as Lancaster's,
With wounded peace which each had prick'd to death.
'Not proven' Averill said, or laughingly
'Some other race of Averills'—prov'n or no,
What cared he? what, if other or the same?
He lean'd not on his fathers but himself.
But Leolin, his brother, living oft
With Averill, and a year or two before
Call'd to the bar, but ever call'd away
By one low voice to one dear neighborhood,
Would often, in his walks with Edith, claim
A distant kinship to the gracious blood
That shook the heart of Edith hearing him.

Sanguine he was: a but less vivid hue
Than of that islet in the chestnut-bloom
Flamed his cheek; and eager eyes, that still
Took joyful note of all things joyful, beam'd,
Beneath a manelike mass of rolling gold,
Their best and brightest, when they dwelt on hers.
Edith, whose pensive beauty, perfect else,
But subject to the season or the mood,
Shone like a mystic star between the less
And greater glory varying to and fro,
We know not wherefore; bounteously made,
And yet so finely, that a troublous touch

Thinn'd, or would seem to thin her in a day,
A joyous to dilate, as toward the light.
And these had been together from the first.
Leolin's first nurse was, five years after, hers:
So much the boy foreran; but when his date
Doubled her own, for want of playmates, he
(Since Averill was a decad and a half
His elder, and their parents underground)
Had tost his ball and flown his kite, and roll'd
His hoop to pleasure Edith, with her dipt
Against the rush of the air in the prone swing,
Made blossom-ball or daisy-chain, arranged
Her garden, sow'd her name and kept it green
In living letters, told her fairy-tales,
Show'd here the fairy footings on the grass,
The little dells of cowslip, fairy palms,
The petty marestail forest, fairy pines,
Or from the tiny pitted target blew
What look'd a flight of fairy arrows aim'd
All at one mark, all hitting: make-believes
For Edith and himself: or else he forged,
But that was later, boyish histories
Of battle, bold adventure, dungeon, wreck,
Flights, terrors, sudden rescues, and true love
Crown'd after trial; sketches rude and faint,
But where a passion yet unborn perhaps
Lay hidden as the music of the moon
Sleeps in the plain eggs of the nightingale.
And thus together, save for college-times
Or Temple-eaten terms, a couple, fair
As ever painter painted, poet sang,
Or Heav'n in lavish bounty moulded, grew.
And more and more, the maiden woman-grown,
He wasted hours with Averill; there, when first
The tented winter-field was broken up
Into that phalanx of the summer spears
That soon should wear the garland; there again
When burr and bine were gather'd; lastly there
At Christmas; ever welcome at the Hall,

On whose dull sameness his full tide of youth
Broke with a phosphorescence cheering even
My lady; and the Baronet yet had laid
No bar between them: dull and self-involved,
Tall and erect, but bending from his height
With half-allowing smiles for all the world,
And mighty courteous in the main—his pride
Lay deeper than to wear it as his ring—
He, like an Aylmer in his Aylmerism,
Would care no more for Leolin's walking with her
Than for his old Newfoundland's, when they ran
To loose him at the stables, for he rose
Twofooted at the limit of his chain,
Roaring to make a third: and how should Love,
Whom the cross-lightnings of four chance-met eyes
Flash into fiery life from nothing, follow
Such dear familiarities of dawn?
Seldom, but when he does, Master of all.

So these young hearts not knowing that they loved,
Not she at least, nor conscious of a bar
Between them, nor by plight or broken ring
Bound, but an immemorial intimacy,
Wander'd at will, but oft accompanied
By Averill: his, a brother's love, that hung
With wings of brooding shelter o'er her peace,
Might have been other, save for Leolin's—
Who knows? but so they wander'd, hour by hour
Gather'd the blossom that rebloom'd, and drank
The magic cup that fill'd itself anew.

A whisper half reveal'd her to herself.
For out beyond her lodges, where the brook
Vocal, with here and there a silence, ran
By sallowy rims, arose the laborers' homes,
A frequent haunt of Edith, on low knolls
That dimpling died into each other, huts
At random scatter'd, each a nest in bloom.

Her art, her hand, her counsel all had wrought
About them: here was one that, summer-blanch'd,
Was parcel-bearded with the traveller's-joy
In Autumn, parcel ivy-clad; and here
The warm-blue breathings of a hidden hearth
Broke from a bower of vine and honeysuckle:
One look'd all rosetree, and another wore
A close-set robe of jasmine sown with stars:
This had a rosy sea of gillyflowers
About it; this, a milky-way on earth,
Like visions in the Northern dreamer's heavens,
A lily-avenue climbing to the doors;
One, almost to the martin-haunted eaves
A summer burial deep in hollyhocks;
Each, its own charm; and Edith's everywhere;
And Edith ever visitant with him,
He but less loved than Edith, of her poor:
For she—so lowly-lovely and so loving,
Queenly responsive when the loyal hand
Rose from the clay it work'd in as she past,
Not sowing hedgerow texts and passing by,
Nor dealing goodly counsel from a height
That makes the lowest hate it, but a voice
Of comfort and an open hand of help,
A splendid presence flattering the poor roofs
Revered as theirs, but kindlier than themselves
To ailing wife or wailing infancy
Or old bedridden palsy,—was adored;
He, loved for her and for himself. A grasp
Having the warmth and muscle of the heart,
A childly way with children, and a laugh
Ringing like proved golden coinage true,
Were no false passport to that easy realm,
Where once with Leolin at her side the girl,
Nursing a child, and turning to the warmth
The tender pink five-beaded baby-soles,
Heard the good mother softly whisper 'Bless,
God bless 'em; marriages are made in Heaven.'

A flash of semi-jealousy clear'd it to her.
My Lady's Indian kinsman unannounced
With half a score of swarthy faces came.
His own, tho' keen and bold and soldierly,
Sear'd by the close ecliptic, was not fair;
Fairer his talk, a tongue that ruled the hour,
Tho' seeming boastful: so when first he dash'd
Into the chronicle of a deedful day,
Sir Aylmer half forgot his lazy smile
Of patron 'Good! my lady's kinsman! good!'
My lady with her fingers interlock'd,
And rotatory thumbs on silken knees,
Call'd all her vital spirits into each ear
To listen: unawares they flitted off,
Busying themselves about the flowerage
That stood from our a stiff brocade in which,
The meteor of a splendid season, she,
Once with this kinsman, ah so long ago,
Stept thro' the stately minuet of those days:
But Edith's eager fancy hurried with him
Snatch'd thro' the perilous passes of his life:
Till Leolin ever watchful of her eye
Hated him with a momentary hate.
Wife-hunting, as the rumor ran, was he:
I know not, for he spoke not, only shower'd
His oriental gifts on everyone
And most on Edith: like a storm he came,
And shook the house, and like a storm he went.

Among the gifts he left her (possibly
He flow'd and ebb'd uncertain, to return
When others had been tested) there was one,
A dagger, in rich sheath with jewels on it
Sprinkled about in gold that branch'd itself
Fine as ice-ferns on January panes
Made by a breath. I know not whence at first,
Nor of what race, the work; but as he told
The story, storming a hill-fort of thieves

He got it; for their captain after fight,
His comrades having fought their last below,
Was climbing up the valley; at whom he shot:
Down from the beetling crag to which he clung
Tumbled the tawny rascal at his feet,
This dagger with him, which when now admired
By Edith whom his pleasure was to please,
At once the costly Sahib yielded it to her.

And Leolin, coming after he was gone,
Tost over all her presents petulantly:
And when she show'd the wealthy scabbard, saying
'Look what a lovely piece of workmanship!'
Slight was his answer 'Well—I care not for it:'
Then playing with the blade he prick'd his hand,
'A gracious gift to give a lady, this!'
'But would it be more gracious' ask'd the girl
'Were I to give this gift of his to one
That is no lady?' 'Gracious? No' said he.
'Me?—but I cared not for it. O pardon me,
I seem to be ungraciousness itself.'
'Take it' she added sweetly 'tho' his gift;
For I am more ungracious ev'n than you,
I care not for it either;' and he said
'Why then I love it:' but Sir Aylmer past,
And neither loved nor liked the thing he heard.

The next day came a neighbor. Blues and reds
They talk'd of: blues were sure of it, he thought:
Then of the latest fox—where started—kill'd
In such a bottom: 'Peter had the brush,
My Peter, first:' and did Sir Aylmer know
That great pock-pitten fellow had been caught?
Then made his pleasure echo, hand to hand,
And rolling as it were the substance of it
Between his palms a moment up and down—
'The birds were warm, the birds were warm upon him;
We have him now:' and had Sir Aylmer heard—

Nay, but he must—the land was ringing of it—
This blacksmith-border marriage—one they knew—
Raw from the nursery—who could trust a child?
That cursed France with her egalities!
And did Sir Aylmer (deferentially
With nearing chair and lower'd accent) think—
For people talk'd—that it was wholly wise
To let that handsome fellow Averill walk
So freely with his daughter? people talk'd—
The boy might get a notion into him;
The girl might be entangled ere she knew.
Sir Aylmer Aylmer slowly stiffening spoke:
'The girl and boy, Sir, know their differences!'
'Good' said his friend 'but watch!' and he 'enough,
More than enough, Sir! I can guard my own.'
They parted, and Sir Aylmer Aylmer watch'd.

Pale, for on her the thunders of the house
Had fallen first, was Edith that same night;
Pale as the Jeptha's daughter, a rough piece
Of early rigid color, under which
Withdrawing by the counter door to that
Which Leolin open'd, she cast back upon him
A piteous glance, and vanish'd. He, as one
Caught in a burst of unexpected storm,
And pelted with outrageous epithets,
Turning beheld the Powers of the House
On either side the hearth, indignant; her,
Cooling her false cheek with a featherfan,
Him glaring, by his own stale devil spurr'd,
And, like a beast hard-ridden, breathing hard.
'Ungenerous, dishonorable, base,
Presumptuous! trusted as he was with her,
The sole succeeder to their wealth, their lands,
The last remaining pillar of their house,
The one transmitter of their ancient name,
Their child.' 'Our child!' 'Our heiress!' 'Ours!' for
still,

Like echoes from beyond a hollow, came
Her sicklier iteration. Last he said
'Boy, mark me! for your fortunes are to make.
I swear you shall not make them out of mine.
Now inasmuch as you have practised on her,
Perplext her, made her half forget herself,
Swerve from her duty to herself and us—
Things in an Aylmer deem'd impossible,
Far as we track ourselves—I say that this,—
Else I withdraw favor and countenance
From you and yours for ever—shall you do.
Sir, when you see her—but you shall not see her—
No, you shall write, and not to her, but me:
And you shall say that having spoken with me,
And after look'd into yourself, you find
That you meant nothing—as indeed you know
That you meant nothing. Such as match as this!
Impossible, prodigious!' These were words,
As meted by his measure of himself,
Arguing boundless forbearance: after which,
And Leolin's horror-stricken answer, 'I
So foul a traitor to myself and her,
Never oh never,' for about as long
As the wind-hover hangs in the balance, paused
Sir Aylmer reddening from the storm within,
Then broke all bonds of courtesy, and crying
'Boy, should I find you by my doors again,
My men shall lash you from the like a dog;
Hence!' with a sudden execration drove
The footstool from before him, and arose;
So, stammering 'scoundrel' out of teeth that ground
As in a dreadful dream, while Leolin still
Retreated half-aghast, the fierce old man
Follow'd, and under his own lintel stood
Storming with lifted hands, a hoary face
Meet for the reverence of the hearth, but now,
Beneath a pale and unimpassion'd moon,
Vext with unworthy madness, and deform'd.

Slowly and conscious of the rageful eye
That watch'd him, till he heard the ponderous door
Close, crashing with long echoes thro' the land,
Went Leolin; then, his passions all in flood
And masters of his motion, furiously
Down thro' the bright lawns to his brother's ran,
And foam'd away his heart at Averill's ear:
Whom Averill solaced as he might, amazed:
The man was his, had been his father's, friend:
He must have seen, himself had seen it long;
He must have known, himself had known: besides,
He never yet had set his daughter forth
Here in the woman-markets of the west,
Where our Caucasians let themselves be sold.
Some one, he thought, had slander'd Leolin to him.
'Brother, for I have loved you more as a son
Than brother, let me tell you: I myself—
What is their pretty saying? jilted is it?
Jilted I was: I say it for your peace.
Pain'd, and, as bearing in myself the shame
The woman should have borne, humiliated,
I lived for years a stunted sunless life;
Till after our good parents past away
Watching your growth, I seem'd again to grow.
Leolin, I almost sin in envying you:
The very whitest lamb in all my fold
Loves you: I know her: the worst thought she has
Is whiter even than her pretty hand:
She must prove true: for, brother, where two fight
The strongest wins, and truth and love are strength,
And you are happy: let her parents be.'

But Leolin cried out the more upon them—
Insolent, brainless, heartless! heiress, wealth,
Their wealth, their heiress! wealth enough was theirs
For twenty matches. Were he lord of this,
Why, twenty boys and girls should marry on it,
And forty blest ones bless him, and himself

Be wealthy still, ay wealthier. He believed
This filthy marriage-hindering Mammon made
The harlot of the cities: nature crost
Was mother of the foul adulteries
That saturate soul with body. Name, too! name,
Their ancient name! they MIGHT be proud; its worth
Was being Edith's. Ah, how pale she had look'd
Darling, to-night! they must have rated her
Beyond all tolerance. These old pheasant-lords,
These partridge-breeders of a thousand years,
Who had mildew'd in their thousands, doing nothing
Since Egbert—why, the greater their disgrace!
Fall back upon a name! rest, rot in that!
Not KEEP it noble, make it nobler? fools,
With such a vantage-ground for nobleness!
He had known a man, a quintessence of man,
The life of all—who madly loved—and he,
Thwarted by one of these old father-fools,
Had rioted his life out, and made an end.
He would not do it! her sweet face and faith
Held him from that: but he had powers, he knew it:
Back would he to his studies, make a name,
Name, fortune too: the world should ring of him
To shame these mouldy Aylmers in their graves:
Chancellor, or what is greatest would he be—
'O brother, I am grieved to learn your grief—
Give me my fling, and let me say my say.'

At which, like one that sees his own excess,
And easily forgives it as his own,
He laugh'd; and then was mute; but presently
Wept like a storm: and honest Averill seeing
How low his brother's mood had fallen, fetch'd
His richest beeswing from a binn reserved
For banquets, praised the waning red, and told
The vintage—when THIS Aylmer came of age—
Then drank and past it; till at length the two,
Tho' Leolin flamed and fell again, agreed

That much allowance must be made for men.
After an angry dream this kindlier glow
Faded with morning, but his purpose held.

Yet once by night again the lovers met,
A perilous meeting under the tall pines
That darken'd all the northward of her Hall.
Him, to her meek and modest bosom prest
In agony, she promised that no force,
Persuasion, no, nor death could alter her:
He, passionately hopefuller, would go,
Labor for his own Edith, and return
In such a sunlight of prosperity
He should not be rejected. 'Write to me!
They loved me, and because I love their child
They hate me: there is war between us, dear,
Which breaks all bonds but ours; we must remain
Sacred to one another.' So they talk'd,
Poor children, for their comfort: the wind blew;
The rain of heaven, and their own bitter tears,
Tears, and the careless rain of heaven, mixt
Upon their faces, as they kiss'd each other
In darkness, and above them roar'd the pine.

So Leolin went; and as we task ourselves
To learn a language known but smatteringly
In phrases here and there at random, toil'd
Mastering the lawless science of our law,
That codeless myriad of precedent,
That wilderness of single instances,
Thro' which a few, by wit or fortune led,
May beat a pathway out to wealth and fame.
The jests, that flash'd about the pleader's room,
Lightning of the hour, the pun, the scurrilous tale,—
Old scandals buried now seven decads deep
In other scandals that have lived and died,
And left the living scandal that shall die—
Were dead to him already; bent as he was

To make disproof of scorn, and strong in hopes,
And prodigal of all brain-labor he,
Charier of sleep, and wine and exercise,
Except when for a breathing-while at eve,
Some niggard fraction of an hour, he ran
Beside the river-bank: and then indeed
Harder the times were, and the hands of power
Were bloodier, and the according hearts of men
Seem'd harder too; but the soft river-breeze,
Which fann'd the gardens of that rival rose
Yet fragrant in a heart remembering
His former talks with Edith, on him breathed
Far purelier in his rushings to and fro,
After his books, to flush his blood with air,
Then to his books again. My lady's cousin,
Half-sickening of his pension'd afternoon,
Drove in upon the student once or twice,
Ran a Malayan muck against the times,
Had golden hopes for France and all mankind,
Answer'd all queries touching those at home
With a heaved shoulder and a saucy smile,
And fain had haled him out into the world,
And air'd him there: his nearer friend would say
'Screw not the chord too sharply lest it snap.'
Then left alone he pluck'd her dagger forth
From where his worldless heart had kept it warm,
Kissing his vows upon it like a knight.
And wrinkled benchers often talk'd of him
Approvingly, and prophesied his rise:
For heart, I think, help'd head: her letters too,
Tho' far between, and coming fitfully
Like broken music, written as she found
Or made occasion, being strictly watch'd,
Charm'd him thro' every labyrinth till he saw
An end, a hope, a light breaking upon him.

But they that cast her spirit into flesh,
Her worldy-wise begetters, plagued themselves

To sell her, those good parents, for her good.
Whatever eldest-born of rank or wealth
Might lie within their compass, him they lured
Into their net made pleasant by the baits
Of gold and beauty, wooing him to woo.
So month by month the noise about their doors,
And distant blaze of those dull banquets, made
The nightly wirer of their innocent hare
Falter before he took it. All in vain.
Sullen, defiant, pitying, wroth, return'd
Leolin's rejected rivals from their suit
So often, that the folly taking wings
Slipt o'er those lazy limits down the wind
With rumor, and became in other fields
A mockery to the yeomen over ale,
And laughter to their lords: but those at home,
As hunters round a hunted creature draw
The cordon close and closer toward the death,
Narrow'd her goings out and comings in;
Forbad her first the house of Averill,
Then closed her access to the wealthiest farms,
Last from her own home-circle of the poor
They barr'd her: yet she bore it: yet her cheek
Kept color: wondrous! but, O mystery!
What amulet drew her down to that old oak,
So old, that twenty years before, a part
Falling had let appear the brand of John—
Once grovelike, each huge arm a tree, but now
The broken base of a black tower, a cave
Of touchwood, with a single flourishing spray.
There the manorial lord too curiously
Raking in that millenial touchwood-dust
Found for himself a bitter treasure-trove;
Burst his own wyvern on the seal, and read
Writhing a letter from his child, for which
Came at the moment Leolin's emissary,
A crippled lad, and coming turn'd to fly,
But scared with threats of jail and halter gave
To him that fluster'd his poor parish wits

The letter which he brought, and swore besides
To play their go-between as heretofore
Nor let them know themselves betray'd, and then,
Soul-stricken at their kindness to him, went
Hating his own lean heart and miserable.

Thenceforward oft from out a despot dream
Panting he woke, and oft as early as dawn
Aroused the black republic on his elms,
Sweeping the frothfly from the fescue, brush'd
Thro' the dim meadow toward his treasure-trove,
Seized it, took home, and to my lady, who made
A downward crescent of her minion mouth,
Listless in all despondence, read; and tore,
As if the living passion symbol'd there
Were living nerves to feel the rent; and burnt,
Now chafing at his own great self defied,
Now striking on huge stumbling-blocks of scorn
In babyisms, and dear diminutives
Scatter'd all over the vocabulary
Of such a love as like a chidden babe,
After much wailing, hush'd itself at last
Hopeless of answer: then tho' Averill wrote
And bad him with good heart sustain himself—
All would be well—the lover heeded not,
But passionately restless came and went,
And rustling once at night about the place,
There by a keeper shot at, slightly hurt,
Raging return'd: nor was it well for her
Kept to the garden now, and grove of pines,
Watch'd even there; and one was set to watch
The watcher, and Sir Aylmer watch'd them all,
Yet bitterer from his readings: once indeed,
Warm'd with his wines, or taking pride in her,
She look'd so sweet, he kiss'd her tenderly
Not knowing what possess'd him: that one kiss
Was Leolin's one strong rival upon earth;
Seconded, for my lady follow'd suit,

Seem'd hope's returning rose: and then ensued
A Martin's summer of his faded love,
Or ordeal by kindness; after this
He seldom crost his child without a sneer;
The mother flow'd in shallower acrimonies:
Never one kindly smile, one kindly word:
So that the gentle creature shut from all
Her charitable use, and face to face
With twenty months of silence, slowly lost
Nor greatly cared to lose, her hold on life.
Last, some low fever ranging round to spy
The weakness of a people or a house,
Like flies that haunt a wound, or deer, or men,
Or almost all that is, hurting the hurt—
Save Christ as we believe him—found the girl
And flung her down upon a couch of fire,
Where careless of the household faces near,
And crying upon the name of Leolin,
She, and with her the race of Aylmer, past.

Star to star vibrates light: may soul to soul
Strike thro' a finer element of her own?
So,—from afar,—touch as at once? or why
That night, that moment, when she named his name,
Did the keen shriek 'yes love, yes Edith, yes,'
Shrill, till the comrade of his chambers woke,
And came upon him half-arisen from sleep,
With a weird bright eye, sweating and trembling,
His hair as it were crackling into flames,
His body half flung forward in pursuit,
And his long arms stretch'd as to grasp a flyer:
Nor knew he wherefore he had made the cry;
And being much befool'd and idioted
By the rough amity of the other, sank
As into sleep again. The second day,
My lady's Indian kinsman rushing in,
A breaker of the bitter news from home,
Found a dead man, a letter edged with death

Beside him, and the dagger which himself
Gave Edith, reddn'd with no bandit's blood:
'From Edith' was engraven on the blade.

Then Averill went and gazed upon his death.
And when he came again, his flock believed—
Beholding how the years which are not Time's
Had blasted him—that many thousand days
Were clipt by horror from his term of life.
Yet the sad mother, for the second death
Scarce touch'd her thro' that nearness of the first,
And being used to find her pastor texts,
Sent to the harrow'd brother, praying him
To speak before the people of her child,
And fixt the Sabbath. Darkly that day rose:
Autumn's mock sunshine of the faded woods
Was all the life of it; for hard on these,
A breathless burthen of low-folded heavens
Stifled and chill'd at once: but every roof
Sent out a listener: many too had known
Edith among the hamlets round, and since
The parents' harshness and the hapless loves
And double death were widely murmur'd, left
Their own gray tower, or plain-faced tabernacle,
To hear him; all in mourning these, and those
With blots of it about them, ribbon, glove
Or kerchief; while the church,—one night, except
For greenish glimmerings thro' the lancets,—made
Still paler the pale head of him, who tower'd
Above them, with his hopes in either grave.

Long o'er his bent brows linger'd Averill,
His face magnetic to the hand from which
Livid he pluck'd it forth, and labor'd thro'
His brief prayer-prelude, gave the verse 'Behold,
Your house is left unto you desolate!'
But lapsed into so long a pause again
As half amazed half frighted all his flock:

Then from his height and loneliness of grief
Bore down in flood, and dash'd his angry heart
Against the desolations of the world.

Never since our bad earth became one sea,
Which rolling o'er the palaces of the proud,
And all but those who knew the living God—
Eight that were left to make a purer world—
When since had flood, fire, earthquake, thunder wrought
Such waste and havoc as the idolatries,
Which from the low light of mortality
Shot up their shadows to the Heaven of Heavens,
And worshipt their own darkness as the Highest?
'Gash thyself, priest, and honor thy brute Baal,
And to thy worst self sacrifice thyself,
For with thy worst self hast thou clothed thy God.'
Then came a Lord in no wise like to Baal.
The babe shall lead the lion. Surely now
The wilderness shall blossom as the rose.
Crown thyself, worm, and worship thine own lusts!—
No coarse and blockish God of acreage
Stands at thy gate for thee to grovel to—
Thy God is far diffused in noble groves
And princely halls, and farms, and flowing lawns,
And heaps of living gold that daily grow,
And title-scrolls and gorgeous heraldries.
In such a shape dost thou behold thy God.
Thou wilt not gash thy flesh for HIM; for thine
Fares richly, in fine linen, not a hair
Ruffled upon the scarfskin, even while
The deathless ruler of thy dying house
Is wounded to the death that cannot die;
And tho' thou numberest with the followers
Of One who cried 'leave all and follow me.'
Thee therefore with His light about thy feet,
Thee with His message ringing in thine ears,
Thee shall thy brother man, the Lord from Heaven,
Born of a village girl, carpenter's son,

Wonderful, Prince of peace, the Mighty God,
Count the more base idolater of the two;
Crueller: as not passing thro' the fire
Bodies, but souls—thy children's—thro' the smoke,
The blight of low desires—darkening thine own
To thine own likeness; or if one of these,
Thy better born unhappily from thee,
Should, as by miracle, grow straight and fair—
Friends, I was bid to speak of such a one
By those who most have cause to sorrow for her—
Fairer than Rachel by the palmy well,
Fairer than Ruth among the fields of corn,
Fair as the Angel that said 'hail' she seem'd,
Who entering fill'd the house with sudden light.
For so mine own was brighten'd: where indeed
The roof so lowly but that beam of Heaven
Dawn'd sometime thro' the doorway? whose the babe
Too ragged to be fondled on her lap,
Warm'd at her bosom? The poor child of shame,
The common care whom no one cared for, leapt
To greet her, wasting his forgotten heart,
As with the mother he had never known,
In gambols; for her fresh and innocent eyes
Had such a star of morning in their blue,
That all neglected places of the field
Broke into nature's music when they saw her.
Low was her voice, but won mysterious way
Thro' the seal'd ear to which a louder one
Was all but silence—free of alms her hand—
The hand that robed your cottage-walls with flowers
Has often toil'd to clothe your little ones;
How often placed upon the sick man's brow
Cool'd it, or laid his feverous pillow smooth!
Had you one sorrow and she shared it not?
One burthen and she would not lighten it?
One spiritual doubt she did not soothe?
Or when some heat of difference sparkled out,
How sweetly would she glide between your wraths,
And steal you from each other! for she walk'd

Wearing the light yoke of that Lord of love,
Who still'd the rolling wave of Galilee!
And one—of him I was not bid to speak—
Was always with her, whom you also knew.
Him too you loved, for he was worthy love.
And these had been together from the first;
They might have been together till the last.
Friends, this frail bark of ours, when sorely tried,
May wreck itself without the pilot's guilt,
Without the captain's knowledge: hope with me.
Whose shame is that, if he went hence with shame?
Nor mine the fault, if losing both of these
I cry to vacant chairs and widow'd walls,
"My house is left unto me desolate."

While thus he spoke, his hearers wept; but some,
Sons of the glebe, with other frowns than those
That knit themselves for summer shadow, scowl'd
At their great lord. He, when it seem'd he saw
No pale sheet-lightnings from afar, but fork'd
Of the near storm, and aiming at his head,
Sat anger-charm'd from sorrow, soldierlike,
Erect: but when the preacher's cadence flow'd
Softening thro' all the gentle attributes
Of his lost child, the wife, who watch'd his face,
Paled at a sudden twitch of his iron mouth;
And 'O pray God that he hold up' she thought
'Or surely I shall shame myself and him.'

'Nor yours the blame—for who beside your hearths
Can take her place—if echoing me you cry
"Our house is left unto us desolate?"
But thou, O thou that killest, hadst thou known,
O thou that stonest, hadst thou understood
The things belonging to thy peace and ours!
Is there no prophet but the voice that calls
Doom upon kings, or in the waste 'Repent'?
Is not our own child on the narrow way,

Who down to those that saunter in the broad
Cries 'come up hither,' as a prophet to us?
Is there no stoning save with flint and rock?
Yes, as the dead we weep for testify—
No desolation but by sword and fire?
Yes, as your moanings witness, and myself
Am lonelier, darker, earthlier for my loss.
Give me your prayers, for he is past your prayers,
Not past the living fount of pity in Heaven.
But I that thought myself long-suffering, meek,
Exceeding "poor in spirit"—how the words
Have twisted back upon themselves, and mean
Vileness, we are grown so proud—I wish'd my voice
A rushing tempest of the wrath of God
To blow these sacrifices thro' the world—
Sent like the twelve-divided concubine
To inflame the tribes: but there—out yonder—earth
Lightens from her own central Hell—O there
The red fruit of an old idolatry—
The heads of chiefs and princes fall so fast,
They cling together in the ghastly sack—
The land all shambles—naked marriages
Flash from the bridge, and ever-murder'd France,
By shores that darken with the gathering wolf,
Runs in a river of blood to the sick sea.
Is this a time to madden madness then?
Was this a time for these to flaunt their pride?
May Pharaoh's darkness, folds as dense as those
Which hid the Holiest from the people's eyes
Ere the great death, shroud this great sin from all:
Doubtless our narrow world must canvass it:
O rather pray for those and pity them,
Who thro' their own desire accomplish'd bring
Their own gray hairs with sorrow to the grave—
Who broke the bond which they desired to break,
Which else had link'd their race with times to come—
Who wove coarse webs to snare her purity,
Grossly contriving their dear daughter's good—
Poor souls, and knew not what they did, but sat

Ignorant, devising their own daughter's death!
May not that earthly chastisement suffice?
Have not our love and reverence left them bare?
Will not another take their heritage?
Will there be children's laughter in their hall
For ever and for ever, or one stone
Left on another, or is it a light thing
That I their guest, their host, their ancient friend,
I made by these the last of all my race
Must cry to these the last of theirs, as cried
Christ ere His agony to those that swore
Not by the temple but the gold, and made
Their own traditions God, and slew the Lord,
And left their memories a world's curse — "Behold,
Your house is left unto you desolate?"'

Ended he had not, but she brook'd no more:
Long since her heart had beat remorselessly,
Her crampt-up sorrow pain'd her, and a sense
Of meanness in her unresisting life.
Then their eyes vext her; for on entering
He had cast the curtains of their seat aside —
Black velvet of the costliest — she herself
Had seen to that: fain had she closed them now,
Yet dared not stir to do it, only near'd
Her husband inch by inch, but when she laid,
Wifelike, her hand in one of his, he veil'd
His face with the other, and at once, as falls
A creeper when the prop is broken, fell
The woman shrieking at his feet, and swoon'd.
Then her own people bore along the nave
Her pendent hands, and narrow meagre face
Seam'd with the shallow cares of fifty years:
And here the Lord of all the landscape round
Ev'n to its last horizon, and of all
Who peer'd at him so keenly, follow'd out
Tall and erect, but in the middle aisle
Reel'd, as a footsore ox in crowded ways

Stumbling across the market to his death,
Unpitied; for he groped as blind, and seem'd
Always about to fall, grasping the pews
And oaken finials till he touch'd the door;
Yet to the lychgate, where his chariot stood,
Strode from the porch, tall and erect again.

But nevermore did either pass the gate
Save under pall with bearers. In one month,
Thro' weary and yet wearier hours,
The childless mother went to seek her child;
And when he felt the silence of his house
About him, and the change and not the change,
And those fixt eyes of painted ancestors
Staring for ever from their gilded walls
On him their last descendant, his own head
Began to droop, to fall; the man became
Imbecile; his one word was 'desolate';
Dead for two years before his death was he;
But when the second Christmas came, escaped
His keepers, and the silence which he felt,
To find a deeper in the narrow gloom
By wife and child; nor wanted at his end
The dark retinue reverencing death
At golden thresholds; nor from tender hearts,
And those who sorrow'd o'er a vanish'd race,
Pity, the violet on the tyrant's grave.
Then the great Hall was wholly broken down,
And the broad woodland parcell'd into farms;
And where the two contrived their daughter's good,
Lies the hawk's cast, the mole has made his run,
The hedgehog underneath the plaintain bores,
The rabbit fondles his own harmless face,
The slow-worm creeps, and the thin weasel there
Follows the mouse, and all is open field.

SEA DREAMS.

SEA DREAMS.

– – –<>– – –

A city clerk, but gently born and bred;
His wife, an unknown artist's orphan child—
One babe was theirs, a Margaret, three years old:
They, thinking that her clear germander eye
Droopt in the giant-factoried city-gloom,
Came, with a month's leave given them, to the sea:
For which his gains were dock'd, however small:
Small were his gains, and hard his work; besides,
Their slender household fortunes (for the man
Had risk'd his little) like the little thrift,
Trembled in perilous places o'er a deep:
And oft, when sitting all alone, his face
Would darken, as he cursed his credulousness,
And that one unctuous mount which lured him, rogue,
To buy strange shares in some Peruvian mine.
Now seaward-bound for health they gain'd a coast,
All sand and cliff and deep-inrunning cave,
At close of day; slept, woke, and went the next,
The Sabbath, pious variers from the church,
To chapel; where a heated pulpiteer,
Not preaching simple Christ to simple men,
Announced the coming doom, and fulminated
Against the scarlet woman and her creed:
For sideways up he swung his arms, and shriek'd

'Thus, thus with violence,' ev'n as if he held
The Apocalyptic millstone, and himself
Were that great Angel; 'Thus with violence
Shall Babylon be cast into the sea;
Then comes the close.' The gentle-hearted wife
Sat shuddering at the ruin of a world;
He at his own: but when the wordy storm
Had ended, forth they came and paced the shore,
Ran in and out the long sea-framing caves,
Drank the large air, and saw, but scarce believed
(The sootflake of so many a summer still
Clung to their fancies) that they saw, the sea.
So now on sand they walk'd, and now on cliff,
Lingering about the thymy promontories,
Till all the sails were darken'd in the west,
And rosed in the east: then homeward and to bed:
Where she, who kept a tender Christian hope
Haunting a holy text, and still to that
Returning, as the bird returns, at night,
'Let not the sun go down upon your wrath,'
Said, 'Love, forgive him:' but he did not speak;
And silenced by that silence lay the wife,
Remembering her dear Lord who died for all,
And musing on the little lives of men,
And how they mar this little by their feuds.

But while the two were sleeping, a full tide
Rose with ground-swell, which, on the foremost rocks
Touching, upjetted in spirts of wild sea-smoke,
And scaled in sheets of wasteful foam, and fell
In vast sea-cataracts—ever and anon
Dead claps of thunder from within the cliffs
Heard thro' the living roar. At this the babe,
Their Margaret cradled near them, wail'd and woke
The mother, and the father suddenly cried,
'A wreck, a wreck!' then turn'd, and groaning said,

'Forgive! How many will say, "forgive," and find
A sort of absolution in the sound
To hate a little longer! No; the sin
That neither God nor man can well forgive,
Hypocrisy, I saw it in him at once.
Is it so true that second thoughts are best?
Not first, and third, which are a riper first?
Too ripe, too late! they come too late for use.
Ah love, there surely lives in man and beast
Something divine to warn them of their foes:
And such a sense, when first I fronted him,
Said, "trust him not;" but after, when I came
To know him more, I lost it, knew him less;
Fought with what seem'd my own uncharity;
Sat at his table; drank his costly wines;
Made more and more allowance for his talk;
Went further, fool! and trusted him with all,
All my poor scrapings from a dozen years
Of dust and deskwork: there is no such mine,
None; but a gulf of ruin, swallowing gold,
Not making. Ruin'd! ruin'd! the sea roars
Ruin: a fearful night!'

'Not fearful; fair,'
Said the good wife, 'if every star in heaven
Can make it fair: you do but bear the tide.
Had you ill dreams?'

'O yes,' he said, 'I dream'd
Of such a tide swelling toward the land,
And I from out the boundless outer deep
Swept with it to the shore, and enter'd one
Of those dark caves that run beneath the cliffs.
I thought the motion of the boundless deep
Bore through the cave, and I was heaved upon it
In darkness: then I saw one lovely star
Larger and larger. "What a world," I thought,
"To live in!" but in moving I found

Only the landward exit of the cave,
Bright with the sun upon the stream beyond:
And near the light a giant woman sat,
All over earthy, like a piece of earth,
A pickaxe in her hand: then out I slipt
Into a land all of sun and blossom, trees
As high as heaven, and every bird that sings:
And here the night-light flickering in my eyes
Awoke me.'

'That was then your dream,' she said,
'Not sad, but sweet.'

'So sweet, I lay,' said he,
'And mused upon it, drifting up the stream
In fancy, till I slept again, and pieced
The broken vision; for I dream'd that still
The motion of the great deep bore me on,
And that the woman walk'd upon the brink:
I wonder'd at her strength, and ask'd her of it:
"It came," she said, "by working in the mines:"
O then to ask her of my shares, I thought;
And ask'd; but not a word; she shook her head.
And then the motion of the current ceased,
And there was rolling thunder; and we reach'd
A mountain, like a wall of burs and thorns;
But she with her strong feet up the steep hill
Trod out a path: I follow'd; and at top
She pointed seaward: there a fleet of glass,
That seem'd a fleet of jewels under me,
Sailing along before a gloomy cloud
That not one moment ceased to thunder, past
In sunshine: right across its track there lay,
Down in the water, a long reef of gold,
Or what seem'd gold: and I was glad at first
To think that in our often-ransack'd world
Still so much gold was left; and then I fear'd
Lest the gay navy there should splinter on it,

And fearing waved my arm to warn them off;
An idle signal, for the brittle fleet
(I thought I could have died to save it) near'd,
Touch'd, clink'd, and clash'd, and vanish'd, and I woke,
I heard the clash so clearly. Now I see
My dream was Life; the woman honest Work;
And my poor venture but a fleet of glass
Wreck'd on a reef of visionary gold.'

'Nay,' said the kindly wife to comfort him,
'You raised your arm, you tumbled down and broke
The glass with little Margaret's medicine it it;
And, breaking that, you made and broke your dream:
A trifle makes a dream, a trifle breaks.'

'No trifle,' groan'd the husband; 'yesterday
I met him suddenly in the street, and ask'd
That which I ask'd the woman in my dream.
Like her, he shook his head. "Show me the books!"
He dodged me with a long and loose account.
"The books, the books!" but he, he could not wait,
Bound on a matter he of life and death:
When the great Books (see Daniel seven and ten)
Were open'd, I should find he meant me well;
And then began to bloat himself, and ooze
All over with the fat affectionate smile
That makes the widow lean. "My dearest friend,
Have faith, have faith! We live by faith," said he;
"And all things work together for the good
Of those"—it makes me sick to quote him—last
Gript my hand hard, and with God-bless-you went.
I stood like one that had received a blow:
I found a hard friend in his loose accounts,
A loose one in the hard grip of his hand,
A curse in his God-bless-you: then my eyes
Pursued him down the street, and far away,
Among the honest shoulders of the crowd,
Read rascal in the motions of his back,

And scoundrel in the supple-sliding knee.'

'Was he so bound, poor soul?' said the good wife;
'So are we all: but do not call him, love,
Before you prove him, rogue, and proved, forgive.
His gain is loss; for he that wrongs his friend
Wrongs himself more, and ever bears about
A silent court of justice in his breast,
Himself the judge and jury, and himself
The prisoner at the bar, ever condemn'd:
And that drags down his life: then comes what comes
Hereafter: and he meant, he said he meant,
Perhaps he meant, or partly meant, you well.'

'"With all his conscience and one eye askew"—
Love, let me quote these lines, that you may learn
A man is likewise counsel for himself,
Too often, in that silent court of yours—
"With all his conscience and one eye askew,
So false, he partly took himself for true;
Whose pious talk, when most his heart was dry,
Made wet the crafty crowsfoot round his eye;
Who, never naming God except for gain,
So never took that useful name in vain;
Made Him his catspaw and the Cross his tool,
And Christ the bait to trap his dupe and fool;
Nor deeds of gift, but gifts of grace he forged,
And snakelike slimed his victim ere he gorged;
And oft at Bible meetings, o'er the rest
Arising, did his holy oily best,
Dropping the too rough H in Hell and Heaven,
To spread the Word by which himself had thriven."
How like you this old satire?'

'Nay,' she said
'I loathe it: he had never kindly heart,
Nor ever cared to better his own kind,

Who first wrote satire, with no pity in it.
But will you hear MY dream, for I had one
That altogether went to music? Still
It awed me.'

Then she told it, having dream'd
Of that same coast.

—But round the North, a light,
A belt, it seem'd, of luminous vapor, lay,
And ever in it a low musical note
Swell'd up and died; and, as it swell'd, a ridge
Of breaker issued from the belt, and still
Grew with the growing note, and when the note
Had reach'd a thunderous fullness, on those cliffs
Broke, mixt with awful light (the same as that
Living within the belt) whereby she saw
That all those lines of cliffs were cliffs no more,
But huge cathedral fronts of every age,
Grave, florid, stern, as far as eye could see.
One after one: and then the great ridge drew,
Lessening to the lessening music, back,
And past into the belt and swell'd again
Slowly to music: ever when it broke
The statues, king or saint, or founder fell;
Then from the gaps and chasms of ruin left
Came men and women in dark clusters round,
Some crying, "Set them up! they shall not fall!"
And others "Let them lie, for they have fall'n."
And still they strove and wrangled: and she grieved
In her strange dream, she knew not why, to find
Their wildest wailings never out of tune
With that sweet note; and ever as their shrieks
Ran highest up the gamut, that great wave
Returning, while none mark'd it, on the crowd
Broke, mixt with awful light, and show'd their eyes
Glaring, and passionate looks, and swept away
The men of flesh and blood, and men of stone,

To the waste deeps together.

'Then I fixt
My wistful eyes on two fair images,
Both crown'd with stars and high among the stars,—
The Virgin Mother standing with her child
High up on one of those dark minster-fronts—
Till she began to totter, and the child
Clung to the mother, and sent out a cry
Which mixt with little Margaret's, and I woke,
And my dream awed me:—well—but what are dreams?
Yours came but from the breaking of a glass,
And mine but from the crying of a child.'

'Child? No!' said he, 'but this tide's roar, and his,
Our Boanerges with his threats of doom,
And loud-lung'd Antibabylonianisms
(Altho' I grant but little music there)
Went both to make your dream: but if there were
A music harmonizing our wild cries,
Sphere-music such as that you dream'd about,
Why, that would make our passions far too like
The discords dear to the musician. No—
One shriek of hate would jar all the hymns of heaven:
True Devils with no ear, they howl in tune
With nothing but the Devil!'

'"True" indeed!
One of our town, but later by an hour
Here than ourselves, spoke with me on the shore;
While you were running down the sands, and made
The dimpled flounce of the sea-furbelow flap,
Good man, to please the child. She brought strange news.
Why were you silent when I spoke to-night?
I had set my heart on your forgiving him
Before you knew. We MUST forgive the dead.'

'Dead! who is dead?'

'The man your eye pursued.
A little after you had parted with him,
He suddenly dropt dead of heart-disease.'

'Dead? he? of heart-disease? what heart had he
To die of? dead!'

'Ah, dearest, if there be
A devil in man, there is an angel too,
And if he did that wrong you charge him with,
His angel broke his heart. But your rough voice
(You spoke so loud) has roused the child again.
Sleep, little birdie, sleep! will she not sleep
Without her "little birdie?" well then, sleep,
And I will sing you "birdie."'

Saying this,
The woman half turn'd round from him she loved,
Left him one hand, and reaching thro' the night
Her other, found (for it was close beside)
And half embraced the basket cradle-head
With one soft arm, which, like the pliant bough
That moving moves the nest and nestling, sway'd
The cradle, while she sang this baby song.

What does the little birdie say
In her nest at peep of day?
Let me fly, says little birdie,
Mother, let me fly away.
Birdie, rest a little longer,
Till the little wings are stronger.
So she rests a little longer,
Then she flies away.

What does little baby say,
In her bed at peep of day?
Baby says, like little birdie,
Let me rise and fly away.
Baby, sleep a little longer,
Till the little limbs are stronger.
If she sleeps a little longer,
Baby too shall fly away.

'She sleeps: let us too, let all evil, sleep.
He also sleeps—another sleep than ours.
He can do no more wrong: forgive him, dear,
And I shall sleep the sounder!'

Then the man,
'His deeds yet live, the worst is yet to come.
Yet let your sleep for this one night be sound:
I do forgive him!'

'Thanks, my love,' she said,
'Your own will be the sweeter,' and they slept.

THE GRANDMOTHER.

THE GRANDMOTHER.

— — —-<>— — —-

I.

And Willy, my eldest-born, is gone, you say, little Anne?
Ruddy and white, and strong on his legs, he looks like a man.
And Willy's wife has written: she never was over-wise,
Never the wife for Willy: he would n't take my advice.

II.

For, Annie, you see, her father was not the man to save,
Had n't a head to manage, and drank himself into his grave.
Pretty enough, very pretty! but I was against it for one.
Eh!—but he would n't hear me—and Willy, you say, is gone.

III.

Willy, my beauty, my eldest-born, the flower of the flock;
Never a man could fling him: for Willy stood like a

rock.
'Here's a leg for a babe of a week!' says doctor; and
he would be bound,
There was not his like that year in twenty parishes
round.

IV.

Strong of his hands, and strong on his legs, but still of
his tongue!
I ought to have gone before him: I wonder he went
so young.
I cannot cry for him, Annie: I have not long to
stay;
Perhaps I shall see him the sooner, for he lived far
away.

V.

Why do you look at me, Annie? you think I am hard
and cold;
But all my children have gone before me, I am so
old:
I cannot weep for Willy, nor can I weep for the
rest;
Only at your age, Annie, I could have wept with the
best.

VI.

For I remember a quarrel I had with your father, my
dear,
All for a slanderous story, that cost me many a
tear.
I mean your grandfather, Annie: it cost me a world
of woe,
Seventy years ago, my darling, seventy years
ago.

VII.

For Jenny, my cousin, had come to the place, and I knew right well
That Jenny had tript in her time: I knew, but I would not tell.
And she to be coming and slandering me, the base little liar!
But the tongue is a fire as you know, my dear, the tongue is a fire.

VIII.

And the parson made it his text that week, and he said likewise,
That a lie which is half a truth is ever the blackest of lies,
That a lie which is all a lie may be met and fought with outright,
But a lie which is part a truth is a harder matter to fight.

IX.

And Willy had not been down to the farm for a week and a day;
And all things look'd half-dead, tho' it was the middle of May.
Jenny, to slander me, who knew what Jenny had been!
But soiling another, Annie, will never make oneself clean.

X.

And I cried myself well-nigh blind, and all of an evening late
I climb'd to the top of the garth, and stood by the road at the gate.
The moon like a rick on fire was rising over the dale,

And whit, whit, whit, in the bush beside me chirrupt
the nightingale.

XI.

All of a sudden he stopt: there past by the gate of
the farm,
Willy,—he did n't see me,—and Jenny hung on his
arm.
Out into the road I started, and spoke I scarce knew
how;
Ah, there's no fool like the old one—it makes me
angry now.

XII.

Willy stood up like a man, and look'd the thing that
he meant;
Jenny, the viper, made me a mocking courtesy and
went.
And I said, 'Let us part: in a hundred years it'll all
be the same,
You cannot love me at all, if you love not my good
name.'

XIII.

And he turn'd, and I saw his eyes all wet, in the sweet
moonshine:
Sweetheart, I love you so well that your good name
is mine.
And what do I care for Jane, let her speak of you well
of ill;
But marry me out of hand: we two shall be happy
still.'

XIV.

'Marry you, Willy!' said I, 'but I needs must speak
my mind,
And I fear you'll listen to tales, be jealous and hard

and unkind.'
But he turn'd and claspt me in his arms, and answer'd,
'No, love, no;'
Seventy years ago, my darling, seventy years
ago.

XV.

So Willy and I were wedded: I wore a lilac
gown;
And the ringers rang with a will, and he gave the
ringers a crown.
But the first that ever I bare was dead before he was
born,
Shadow and shine is life, little Annie, flower and
thorn.

XVI.

That was the first time, too, that ever I thought of
death.
There lay the sweet little body that never had drawn
a breath.
I had not wept, little Anne, not since I had been a
wife;
But I wept like a child that day, for the babe had
fought for his life.

XVII.

His dear little face was troubled, as if with anger or
pain:
I look'd at the still little body—his trouble had all
been in vain.
For Willy I cannot weep, I shall see him another
morn:
But I wept like a child for the child that was dead
before he was born.

XVIII.

But he cheer'd me, my good man, for he seldom said me nay:
Kind, like a man, was he; like a man, too, would have his way:
Never jealous—not he: we had many a happy year;
And he died, and I could not weep—my own time seem'd so near.

XIX.

But I wish'd it had been God's will that I, too, then could have died:
I began to be tired a little, and fain had slept at his side.
And that was ten years back, or more, if I don't forget:
But as to the children, Annie, they're all about me yet.

XX.

Pattering over the boards, my Annie who left me at two,
Patter she goes, my own little Annie, an Annie like you:
Pattering over the boards, she comes and goes at her will,
While Harry is in the five-acre and Charlie ploughing the hill.

XXI.

And Harry and Charlie, I hear them too—they sing to their team:
Often they come to the door in a pleasant kind of a dream.
They come and sit by my chair, they hover about my bed—

I am not always certain if they be alive or
dead.

XXII.

And yet I know for a truth, there's none of them
left alive;
For Harry went at sixty, your father at sixty-five:
And Willy, my eldest born, at nigh threescore and
ten;
I knew them all as babies, and now they're elderly
men.

XXIII.

For mine is a time of peace, it is not often I
grieve;
I am oftener sitting at home in my father's farm
at eve:
And the neighbors come and laugh and gossip, and
so do I;
I find myself often laughing at things that have long
gone by.

XXIV.

To be sure the preacher says, our sins should make
us sad:
But mine is a time of peace, and there is Grace to
be had;
And God, not man, is the Judge of us all when life
shall cease;
And in this Book, little Annie, the message is one of
Peace.

XXV.

And age is a time of peace, so it be free from
pain,
And happy has been my life; but I would not live
it again.

I seem to be tired a little, that's all, and long for
rest;
Only at your age, Annie, I could have wept with the
best.

XXVI.

So Willy has gone, my beauty, my eldest-born, my
flower;
But how can I weep for Willy, he has but gone for
an hour,—
Gone for a minute, my son, from this room into the
next;
I, too, shall go in a minute. What time have I to
be vext?

XXVII.

And Willy's wife has written, she never was over-wise.
Get me my glasses, Annie: thank God that I keep
my eyes.
There is but a trifle left you, when I shall have past
away.
But stay with the old woman now: you cannot have
long to stay.

NORTHERN FARMER.

NORTHERN FARMER.
old style.
— — —-<>— — —-

I.

Wheer 'asta bean saw long and mea liggin' 'ere aloan?
Noorse? thoort nowt o' a noorse: whoy, doctor's abean an' agoan:
Says that I moant 'a naw moor yaale: but I beant a fool:
Git ma my yaale, fur I beant a-gooin' to break my rule.

II.

Doctors, they knaws nowt, for a says what's nawways true:
Naw soort o' koind o' use to saay the things that a do.
I've 'ed my point o' yaale ivry noight sin' I bean 'ere,
An' I've 'ed my quart ivry market-noight for foorty year.

III.

Parson's a bean loikewoise, an' a sittin' ere o' my

bed.
'The amoighty's a taakin o' you to 'issen, my friend,'
'a said,
An' a towd ma my sins, an's toithe were due, an' I gied
it in hond;
I done my duty by un, as I 'a done by the
lond.

IV.

Larn'd a ma' bea. I reckons I 'annot sa mooch to
larn.
But a cost oop, thot a did, 'boot Bessy Marris's
barn.
Thof a knaws I hallus voated wi' Squoire an' choorch
an staate,
An' i' the woost o' toimes I wur niver agin the
raate.

V.

An' I hallus comed to 's choorch afoor moy Sally wur
dead,
An' 'eerd un a bummin' awaay loike a buzzard-clock*
ower my yead,
An' I niver knaw'd whot a mean'd but I thowt a 'ad
summut to saay,
An I thowt a said whot a owt to 'a said an' I comed
awaay.

*Cockchafer.

VI.

Bessy Marris's barn! tha knaws she laaid it to
mea.
Mowt 'a bean, mayhap, for she wur a bad un,
shea.
'Siver, I kep un, I kep un, my lass, tha mun under-stond;
I done my duty by un as I 'a done by the

lond.

VII.

But Parson a comes an' a goos, an' a says it easy an' freea
'The amoighty's a taakin o' you to 'issen, my friend,' says 'ea.
I weant saay men be loiars, thof summun said it in 'aaste:
But a reads wonn sarmin a weeak, an' I 'a stubb'd Thornaby waaste.

VIII.

D'ya moind the waaste, my lass? naw, naw, tha was not born then;
Theer wur a boggle in it, I often 'eerd un mysen;
Moast loike a butter-bump,* for I 'eerd un aboot an aboot,
But I stubb'd un oop wi' the lot, an' raaved an rembled un oot.

*Bittern.

IX.

Keaper's it wur; fo' they fun un theer a laaid on 'is faace
Doon i' the woild 'enemies* afoor I comed to the plaace.
Noaks or Thimbleby—toner 'ed shot un as dead as a naail.
Noaks wur 'ang'd for it oop at 'soize—but git ma my yaale.

*Anenomes.

X.

Dubbut looak at the waaste: theer warn't not fead for a cow:

Nowt at all but bracken an' fuzz, an' looak at it now—
Warn't worth nowt a haacre, an' now theer's lots o' fead,
Fourscore yows upon it an' some on it doon in sead.

XI.

Nobbut a bit on it's left, an' I mean'd to 'a stubb'd it at fall,
Done it ta-year I mean'd, an' runn'd plow thruff it an' all,
If godamoighty an' parson 'ud nobbut let ma aloan,
Mea, wi' haate oonderd haacre o' Squoire's an' lond o' my oan.

XII.

Do godamoighty knaw what a's doing a-taakin' o' mea?
I beant wonn as saws 'ere a bean an' yonder a pea;
An' Squoire 'ull be sa mad an' all—a' dear a' dear!
And I 'a monaged for Squoire come Michaelmas thirty year.

XIII.

A mowt 'a taaken Joanes, as 'ant a 'aapoth o' sense,
Or a mowt a' taaken Robins—a niver mended a fence:
But godamoighty a moost taake mea an' taake ma now
Wi 'auf the cows to cauve an' Thornaby holms to plow!

XIV.

Looak 'ow quoloty smoiles when they sees ma a
passin' by,
Says to thessen naw doot 'what a mon a be
sewer-ly!'
For they knaws what I bean to Squoire sin fust a
comed to the 'All;
I done my duty by Squoire an' I done my duty
by all.

XV.

Squoire's in Lunnon, an' summun I reckons 'ull 'a to
wroite,
For who's to howd the lond ater mea thot muddles
ma quoit;
Sartin-sewer I bea, thot a weant niver give it to
Joanes,
Noither a moant to Robins—a niver rembles the
stoans.

XVI.

But summun 'ull come ater mea mayhap wi' 'is kittle
o' steam
Huzzin' an' maazin' the blessed fealds wi' the Divil's
oan team.
Gin I mun doy I mun doy, an' loife they says is
sweet,
But gin I mun doy I mun doy, for I couldn abear to
see it.

XVII.

What atta stannin' theer for, an' doesn bring ma the
yaale?
Doctor's a 'tottler, lass, an a's hallus i' the owd
taale;
I weant break rules for Doctor, a knaws naw moor
nor a floy;

Git ma my yaale, I tell tha, an' gin I mun doy I mun doy.

MISCELLANEOUS.

TITHONUS.

— —-<>— —-

The woods decay, the woods decay and fall,
The vapors weep their burthen to the ground,
Man comes and tills the field and lies beneath,
And after many a summer dies the swan.
Me only cruel immortality
Consumes: I wither slowly in thine arms,
Here at the quiet limit of the world,
A white-hair'd shadow roaming like a dream
The ever-silent spaces of the East,
Far-folded mists, and gleaming halls of morn.

Alas! for this gray shadow, once a man—
So glorious in his beauty and thy choice,
Who madest him thy chosen, that he seem'd
To his great heart none other than a God!
I ask'd thee, 'Give me immortality.'
Then didst thou grant mine asking with a smile,
Like wealthy men who care not how they give.
But thy strong Hours indignant work'd their wills,
And beat me down and marr'd and wasted me,
And tho' they could not end me, left me maim'd
To dwell in presence of immortal youth,
Immortal age beside immortal youth,

And all I was, in ashes. Can thy love,
Thy beauty, make amends, tho' even now,
Close over us, the silver star, thy guide,
Shines in those tremulous eyes that fill with tears
To hear me? Let me go: take back thy gift:
Why should a man desire in any way
To vary from the kindly race of men,
Or pass beyond the goal of ordinance
Where all should pause, as is most meet for all?

A soft air fans the cloud apart; there comes
A glimpse of that dark world where I was born.
Once more the old mysterious glimmer steals
From thy pure brows, and from thy shoulders pure,
And bosom beating with a heart renew'd.
Thy cheek begins to redden thro' the gloom,
Thy sweet eyes brighten slowly close to mine,
Ere yet they blind the stars, and the wild team
Which love thee, yearning for thy yoke, arise,
And shake the darkness from their loosen'd manes,
And beat the twilight into flakes of fire.

Lo! ever thus thou growest beautiful
In silence, then before thine answer given
Departest, and thy tears are on my cheek.

Why wilt thou ever scare me with thy tears,
And make me tremble lest a saying learnt,
In days far-off, on that dark earth, be true?
'The Gods themselves cannot recall their gifts.'

Ay me! ay me! with what another heart
In days far-off, and with what other eyes
I used to watch—if I be he that watch'd—
The lucid outline forming round thee; saw
The dim curls kindle into sunny rings;
Changed with thy mystic change, and felt my blood

Glow with the glow that slowly crimson'd all
Thy presence and thy portals, while I lay,
Mouth, forehead, eyelids, growing dewy-warm
With kisses balmier than half-opening buds
Of April, and could hear the lips that kiss'd
Whispering I knew not what of wild and sweet,
Like that strange song I heard Apollo sing,
While Ilion like a mist rose into towers.

Yet hold me not for ever in thine East:
How can my nature longer mix with thine?
Coldly thy rosy shadows bathe me, cold
Are all thy lights, and cold my wrinkled feet
Upon thy glimmering thresholds, when the steam
Floats up from those dim fields about the homes
Of happy men that have the power to die,
And grassy barrows of the happier dead.
Release me, and restore me to the ground;
Thou seest all things, thou wilt see my grave:
Thou wilt renew thy beauty morn by morn;
I earth in earth forget these empty courts,
And thee returning on thy silver wheels.

THE VOYAGE.

— —-<>— —-

I.

We left behind the painted buoy
That tosses at the harbor-mouth;
And madly danced our hearts with joy,
As fast we fleeted to the South:
How fresh was every sight and sound
On open main or winding shore!

We knew the merry world was round,
  And we might sail for evermore.

II.

Warm broke the breeze against the brow,
  Dry sang the tackle, sang the sail:
The Lady's-head upon the prow
  Caught the shrill salt, and sheer'd the gale.
The broad seas swell'd to meet the keel,
  And swept behind: so quick the run,
We felt the good ship shake and reel,
  We seem'd to sail into the Sun!

III.

How oft we saw the Sun retire,
  And burn the threshold of the night,
Fall from his Ocean-lane of fire,
  And sleep beneath his pillar'd light!
How oft the purple-skirted robe
  Of twilight slowly downward drawn,
As thro' the slumber of the globe
  Again we dash'd into the dawn!

IV.

New stars all night above the brim
  Of waters lighten'd into view;
They climb'd as quickly, for the rim
  Changed every moment as we flew.
Far ran the naked moon across
  The houseless ocean's heaving field,
Or flying shone, the silver boss
  Of her own halo's dusky shield;

V.

The peaky islet shifted shapes,
  High towns on hills were dimly seen,
We past long lines of Northern capes

And dewy Northern meadows green.
We came to warmer waves, and deep
Across the boundless east we drove,
Where those long swells of breaker sweep
The nutmeg rocks and isles clove.

VI.

By peaks that flamed, or, all in shade,
Gloom'd the low coast and quivering brine
With ashy rains, that spreading made
Fantastic plume or sable pine;
By sands and steaming flats, and floods
Of mighty mouth, we scudded fast,
And hills and scarlet-mingled woods
Glow'd for a moment as we past.

VII.

O hundred shores of happy climes,
How swiftly stream'd ye by the bark!
At times the whole sea burn'd, at times
With wakes of fire we tore the dark;
At times a carven craft would shoot
From havens hid in fairy bowers,
With naked limbs and flowers and fruit,
But we nor paused for fruit nor flowers.

VIII.

For one fair Vision ever fled
Down the waste waters day and night,
And still we follow'd where she led,
In hope to gain upon her flight.
Her face was evermore unseen,
And fixt upon the far sea-line;
But each man murmur'd 'O my Queen,
I follow till I make thee mine.'

IX.

And now we lost her, now she gleam'd
 Like Fancy made of golden air,
Now nearer to the prow she seem'd
 Like Virtue firm, like Knowledge fair,
Now high on waves that idly burst
 Like Heavenly Hope she crown'd the sea
And now, the bloodless point reversed,
 She bore the blade of Liberty.

X.

And only one among us—him
 We please not—he was seldom pleased:
He saw not far: his eyes were dim:
 But ours he swore were all diseased.
'A ship of fools' he shriek'd in spite,
 'A ship of fools' he sneer'd and wept.
And overboard one stormy night
 He cast his body, and on we swept.

XI.

And never sail of ours was furl'd,
 Nor anchor dropt at eve or morn;
We loved the glories of the world,
 But laws of nature were our scorn;
For blasts would rise and rave and cease,
 But whence were those that drove the sail
Across the whirlwind's heart of peace,
 And to and thro' the counter-gale?

XII.

Again to colder climes we came,
 For still we follow'd where she led:
Now mate is blind and captain lame,
 And half the crew are sick or dead.
But blind or lame or sick or sound
 We follow that which flies before:

We know the merry world is round,
 And we may sail for evermore.

IN THE VALLEY OF CAUTERETZ.

— —-<>— —-

All along the valley, stream that flashest white,
Deepening thy voice with the deepening of the night,
All along the valley, where thy waters flow,
I walk'd with one I loved two and thirty years ago.
All along the valley while I walk'd to-day,
The two and thirty years were a mist that rolls away;
For all along the valley, down thy rocky bed
Thy living voice to me was as the voice of the dead,
And all along the valley, by rock and cave and tree,
The voice of the dead was a living voice to me.

THE FLOWER.

— —-<>— —-

Once in a golden hour
 I cast to earth a seed.
Up there came a flower,
 The people said, a weed.

To and fro they went
 Thro' my garden-bower,
And muttering discontent

Cursed me and my flower.

Then it grew so tall
 It wore a crown of light,
But thieves from o'er the wall
 Stole the seed by night.

Sow'd it far and wide
 By every town and tower,
Till all the people cried
 'Splendid is the flower.'

Read my little fable:
 He that runs may read.
Most can raise the flowers now,
 For all have got the seed.

And some are pretty enough,
 And some are poor indeed;
And now again the people
 Call it but a weed.

REQUIESCAT.

— —-<>— —-

Fair is her cottage in its place,
 Where yon broad water sweetly slowly glides.
It sees itself from thatch to base
 Dream in the sliding tides.

And fairer she, but ah how soon to die!
  Her quiet dream of life this hour may cease.
Her peaceful being slowly passes by
  To some more perfect peace.

THE SAILOR BOY.

— — —-<>— — —-

He rose at dawn and, fired with hope,
  Shot o'er the seething harbor-bar,
And reach'd the ship and caught the rope,
  And whistled to the morning star.

And while he whistled long and loud
  He heard a fierce mermaiden cry,
'O boy, tho' thou art young and proud,
  I see the place where thou wilt lie.

'The sands and yeasty surges mix
  In caves about the dreary bay,
And on thy ribs the limpet sticks,
  And in thy heart the scrawl shall play.'

'Fool,' he answer'd, 'death is sure
  To those that stay and those that roam,
But I will nevermore endure
  To sit with empty hands at home.

'My mother clings about my neck,
  My sisters crying "stay for shame;"
My father raves of death and wreck,

They are all to blame, they are all to blame.

'God help me! save I take my part
Of danger in the roaring sea,
A devil rises in my heart,
Far worse than any death to me.'

THE ISLET.

— —<>— —

'Whither O whither love shall we go,
For a score of sweet little summers or so'
The sweet little wife of the singer said,
On the day that follow'd the day she was wed,
'Whither O whither love shall we go?'
And the singer shaking his curly head
Turn'd as he sat, and struck the keys
There at his right with a sudden crash,
Singing, 'and shall it be over the seas
With a crew that is neither rude nor rash,
But a bevy of Eroses apple-cheek'd,
In a shallop of crystal ivory-beak'd,
With a satin sail of a ruby glow,
To a sweet little Eden on earth that I know,
A mountain islet pointed and peak'd;
Waves on a diamond shingle dash,
Cataract brooks to the ocean run,
Fairily-delicate palaces shine
Mixt with myrtle and clad with vine,
And overstream'd and silvery-streak'd
With many a rivulet high against the Sun
The facets of the glorious mountain flash

Above the valleys of palm and pine.'

'Thither O thither, love, let us go.'

'No, no, no!
For in all that exquisite isle, my dear,
There is but one bird with a musical throat,
And his compass is but of a single note,
That it makes one weary to hear.'

'Mock me not! mock me not! love, let us go.'

'No, love, no.
For the bud ever breaks into bloom on the tree,
And a storm never wakes on the lonely sea,
And a worm is there in the lonely wood,
That pierces the liver and blackens the blood,
And makes it a sorrow to be.'

THE RINGLET.

— —-<>— —-

'Your ringlets, your ringlets,
That look so golden-gay,
If you will give me one, but one,
To kiss it night and day,
Then never chilling touch of Time
Will turn it silver-gray;
And then shall I know it is all true gold
To flame and sparkle and stream as of old,
Till all the comets in heaven are cold,
And all her stars decay.'
'Then take it, love, and put it by;

This cannot change, nor yet can I.'

2.

'My ringlet, my ringlet,
  That art so golden-gay,
Now never chilling touch of Time
  Can turn thee silver-gray;
And a lad may wink, and a girl may hint,
  And a fool may say his say;
For my doubts and fears were all amiss,
And I swear henceforth by this and this,
That a doubt will only come for a kiss,
  And a fear to be kiss'd away.'
'Then kiss it, love, and put it by:
If this can change, why so can I.'

II.

O Ringlet, O Ringlet,
  I kiss'd you night and day,
And Ringlet, O Ringlet,
  You still are golden-gay,
But Ringlet, O Ringlet,
  You should be silver-gray:
For what is this which now I'm told,
I that took you for true gold,
She that gave you's bought and sold,
      Sold, sold.

2.

O Ringlet, O Ringlet,
  She blush'd a rosy red,
When Ringlet, O Ringlet,
  She clipt you from her head,
And Ringlet, O Ringlet,
  She gave you me, and said,
'Come, kiss it, love, and put it by

If this can change, why so can I.'
O fie, you golden nothing, fie
          You golden lie.

3.

O Ringlet, O Ringlet,
  I count you much to blame,
For Ringlet, O Ringlet,
  You put me much to shame,
So Ringlet, O Ringlet,
  I doom you to the flame.
For what is this which now I learn,
Has given all my faith a turn?
Burn, you glossy heretic, burn,
          Burn, burn.

A WELCOME TO ALEXANDRA.

March 7, 1863.

— —-<>— —-

Sea-kings' daughter from over the sea,
                              Alexandra!
Saxon and Norman and Dane are we,
But all of us Danes in our welcome of thee,
                              Alexandra!
Welcome her, thunders of fort and of fleet!
Welcome her, thundering cheer of the street!
Welcome her, all things youthful and sweet,
Scatter the blossom under her feet!
Break, happy land, into earlier flowers!
Make music, O bird, in the new-budded bowers!
Blazon your mottos of blessing and prayer!
Welcome her, welcome her, all that is ours!

Warble, O bugle, and trumpet, blare!
Flags, flutter out upon turrets and towers!
Flames, on the windy headland flare!
Utter your jubilee, steeple and spire!
Clash, ye bells, in the merry March air!
Flash, ye cities, in rivers of fire!
Rush to the roof, sudden rocket, and higher
Melt into stars for the land's desire!
Roll and rejoice, jubilant voice,
Roll as a ground-swell dash'd on the strand,
Roar as the sea when he welcomes the land,
And welcome her, welcome the land's desire,
The sea-kings' daughter as happy as fair,
Blissful bride of a blissful heir,
Bride of the heir of the kings of the sea—
O joy to the people and joy to the throne,
Come to us, love us, and make us your own:
For Saxon or Dane or Norman we,
Teuton or Celt, or whatever we be,
We are each all Dane in our welcome of thee,
Alexandra!

ODE
SUNG AT THE OPENING OF THE INTERNATIONAL EXHIBITION.

— —-<>— —-

Uplift a thousand voices full and sweet,
In this wide hall with earth's inventions stored,
And praise th' invisible universal Lord,
Who lets once more in peace the nations meet,
Where Science, Art, and Labor have outpour'd
Their myriad horns of plenty at our feet.

O silent father of our Kings to be
Mourn'd in this golden hour of jubilee,
For this, for all, we weep our thanks to thee!

The world-compelling plan was thine,
And, lo! the long laborious miles
Of Palace; lo! the giant aisles,
Rich in model and design;
Harvest-tool and husbandry,
Loom and wheel and engin'ry,
Secrets of the sullen mine,
Steel and gold, and corn and wine,
Fabric rough, or Fairy fine,
Sunny tokens of the Line,
Polar marvels, and a feast
Of wonder, out of West and East,
And shapes and hues of Part divine!
All of beauty, all of use,
That one fair planet can produce.
Brought from under every star,
Blown from over every main,
And mixt, as life is mixt with pain,
The works of peace with works of war.

O ye, the wise who think, the wise who reign,
From growing commerce loose her latest chain,
And let the fair white-winged peacemaker fly
To happy havens under all the sky,
And mix the seasons and the golden hours,
Till each man finds his own in all men's good,
And all men work in noble brotherhood,
Breaking their mailed fleets and armed towers,
And ruling by obeying Nature's powers,
And gathering all the fruits of peace and crown'd with
all her flowers.

A DEDICATION.

Dear, near and true—no truer Time himself
Can prove you, tho' he make you evermore
Dearer and nearer, as the rapid of life
Shoots to the fall—take this, and pray that he,
Who wrote it, honoring your sweet faith in him,
May trust himself; and spite of praise and scorn,
As one who feels the immeasurable world,
Attain the wise indifference of the wise;
And after Autumn past—if left to pass
His autumn into seeming-leafless days—
Draw toward the long frost and longest night,
Wearing his wisdom lightly, like the fruit
Which in our winter woodland looks a flower.*

*The fruit of the Spindle-tree (Euonymus Europaeus).

EXPERIMENTS.

BOADICEA.

— —-<>— —-

While about the shore of Mona those Neronian legionaries
Burnt and broke the grove and altar of the Druid and Druidess,
Far in the East Boadicea, standing loftily charioted,
Mad and maddening all that heard her in her fierce volubility,
Girt by half the tribes of Britain, near the colony Camulodune,
Yell'd and shriek'd between her daughters o'er a wild confederacy.

'They that scorn the tribes and call us Britain's barbarous populaces,
Did they hear me, would they listen, did they pity me supplicating?
Shall I heed them in their anguish? shall I brook to be supplicated?
Hear Icenian, Catieuchlanian, hear Coritanian, Trinobant!
Must their ever-ravening eagle's beak and talon annihilate us?
Tear the noble hear of Britain, leave it gorily quivering?
Bark an answer, Britain's raven! bark and blacken innumerable,
Blacken round the Roman carrion, make the carcase a skeleton,
Kite and kestrel, wolf and wolfkin, from the wilderness, wallow in it,
Till the face of Bel be brighten'd, Taranis be propitiated.
Lo their colony half-defended! lo their colony, Camulodune!
There the horde of Roman robbers mock at a barbarous adversary.
There the hive of Roman liars worship a gluttonous emperor-idiot.

Such is Rome, and this her deity: hear it, Spirit of Cassivelaun!

'Hear it, Gods! the Gods have heard it, O Icenian, O Coritanian!
Doubt not ye the Gods have answer'd, Catieuchlanian, Trinobant.
These have told us all their anger in miraculous utterances,
Thunder, a flying fire in heaven, a murmur heard aerially,
Phantom sound of blows descending, moan of an enemy massacred,
Phantom wail of women and children, multitudinous agonies.
Bloodily flow'd the Tamesa rolling phantom bodies of horses and men;
Then a phantom colony smoulder'd on the refluent estuary;
Lastly yonder yester-even, suddenly giddily tottering—
There was one who watch'd and told me—down their statue of Victory fell.
Lo their precious Roman bantling, lo the colony Camulodune,
Shall we teach it a Roman lesson? shall we care to be pitiful?
Shall we deal with it as an infant? shall we dandle it amorously?

'Hear Icenian, Catieuchlanian, hear Coritanian, Trinobant!
While I roved about the forest, long and bitterly meditating,
There I heard them in the darkness, at the mystical ceremony,
Loosely robed in flying raiment, sang the terrible prophetesses.
"Fear not, isle of blowing woodland, isle of silvery parapets!
Tho' the Roman eagle shadow thee, tho' the gathering enemy narrow thee,
Thou shalt wax and he shall dwindle, thou shalt be the mighty one yet!
Thine the liberty, thine the glory, thine the deeds to be celebrated,
Thine the myriad-rolling ocean, light and shadow illimitable,
Thine the lands of lasting summer, many-blossoming Paradises,
Thine the North and thine the South and thine the battle-thunder of God."
So they chanted: how shall Britain light upon auguries happier?
So they chanted in the darkness, and there cometh a victory now.

Hear Icenian, Catieuchlanian, hear Coritanian, Trinobant!
Me the wife of rich Prasutagus, me the lover of liberty,
Me they seized and me they tortured, me they lash'd and humiliated,
Me the sport of ribald Veterans, mine of ruffian violators!
See they sit, they hide their faces, miserable in ignominy!
Wherefore in me burns an anger, not by blood to be satiated.
Lo the palaces and the temple, lo the colony Camulodune!
There they ruled, and thence they wasted all the flourishing territory,
Thither at their will they haled the yellow-ringleted Britoness—
Bloodily, bloodily fall the battle-axe, unexhausted, inexorable.
Shout Icenian, Catieuchlanian, shout Coritanian, Trinobant,
Till the victim hear within and yearn to hurry precipitously
Like the leaf in a roaring whirlwind, like the smoke in a hurricane whirl'd.
Lo the colony, there they rioted in the city of Cunobeline!
There they drank in cups of emerald, there at tables of ebony lay,
Rolling on their purple couches in their tender effeminacy.
There they dwelt and there they rioted; there—there—they dwell no more.
Burst the gates, and burn the palaces, break the works of the statuary,
Take the hoary Roman head and shatter it, hold it abominable,
Cut the Roman boy to pieces in his lust and voluptuousness,
Lash the maiden into swooning, me they lash'd and humiliated,
Chop the breasts from off the mother, dash the brains of the little one out,
Up my Britons, on my chariot, on my chargers, trample them under us.'

So the Queen Boadicea, standing loftily charioted,
Brandishing in her hand a dart and rolling glances lioness-like,
Yell'd and shriek'd between her daughters in her fierce volubility.
Till her people all around the royal chariot agitated,
Madly dash'd the darts together, writhing barbarous lineaments,
Made the noise of frosty woodlands, when they shiver in January,
Roar'd as when the rolling breakers boom and blanch on the preci-

pices,
Yell'd as when the winds of winter tear an oak on a promontory.
So the silent colony hearing her tumultuous adversaries
Clash the darts and on the buckler beat with rapid unanimous hand,
Thought on all her evil tyrannies, all her pitiless avarice,
Till she felt the heart within her fall and flutter tremulously,
Then her pulses at the clamoring of her enemy fainted away.
Out of evil evil flourishes, out of tyranny tyranny buds.
Ran the land with Roman slaughter, multitudinous agonies.
Perish'd many a maid and matron, many a valorous legionary.
Fell the colony, city, and citadel, London, Verulam, Camulodune.

IN QUANTITY.

— —-<> — —-

MILTON.

Alcaics.

O mighty-mouth'd inventor of harmonies,
O skill'd to sing of Time or Eternity,
  God-gifted organ-voice of England,
    Milton, a name to resound for ages;
Whose Titan angels, Gabriel, Abdiel,
Starr'd from Jehovah's gorgeous armouries,
  Tower, as the deep-domed empyrean
    Rings to the roar of an angel onset—
Me rather all that bowery loneliness,
The brooks of Eden mazily murmuring,
  And bloom profuse and cedar arches
    Charm, as a wanderer out in ocean,
Where some refulgent sunset of India
Streams o'er a rich ambrosial ocean isle,
  And crimson-hued the stately palmwoods

Whisper in odorous heights of even.

– – – – – – – –

Hendecasyllabics.

O you chorus of indolent reviewers,
Irresponsible, indolent reviewers,
Look, I come to the test, a tiny poem
All composed in a metre of Catullus,
All in quantity, careful of my motion,
Like the skater on ice that hardly bears him,
Lest I fall unawares before the people,
Waking laughter in indolent reviewers.
Should I flounder awhile without a tumble
Thro' this metrification of Catullus,
They should speak to me not without a welcome,
All that chorus of indolent reviewers.
Hard, hard, hard is it, only not to tumble,
So fantastical is the dainty metre.
Wherefore slight me not wholly, nor believe me
Too presumptuous, indolent reviewers.
O blatant Magazines, regard me rather—
Since I blush to belaud myself a moment—
As some rare little rose, a piece of inmost
Horticultural art, or half coquette-like
Maiden, not to be greeted unbenignly.

SPECIMEN OF A TRANSLATION OF THE ILIAD IN BLANK VERSE.

So Hector said, and sea-like roar'd his host;
Then loosed their sweating horses from the yoke,

And each beside his chariot bound his own;
And oxen from the city, and goodly sheep
In haste they drove, and honey-hearted wine
And bread from out the houses brought, and heap'd
Their firewood, and the winds from off the plain
Roll'd the rich vapor far into the heaven.
And these all night upon the[1] bridge of war
Sat glorying; many a fire before them blazed:
As when in heaven the stars about the moon
Look beautiful, when all the winds are laid,
And every height comes out, and jutting peak
And valley, and the immeasurable heavens
Break open to their highest, and all the stars
Shine, and the Shepherd gladdens in his heart:
So many a fire between the ships and stream
Of Xanthus blazed before the towers of Troy,
A thousand on the plain; and close by each
Sat fifty in the blaze of burning fire;
And champing golden grain, the horses stood
Hard by their chariots, waiting for the dawn.[2]
Iliad VIII. 542-561.

[1] Or, ridge.

[2] Or more literally—

And eating hoary grain and pulse the steeds
Stood by their cars, waiting the throned morn.